The Irregular at MagicHigh School

1

Tsutomu Sato

Illustration Kana Ishida

Illustration assistants Jimmy Stone,
Yasuko Suenaga

Design BEE-PEE

"Good morning."

Tatsuya Shiba

The older brother of the Shiba siblings. A new student of the National Magic University Affiliated First High School. Part of Class 1-E. One of the Course 2 students, mockingly called "Weeds." Specializes in designing Casting Assistant Devices (CADs).

"Ja!"

Leonhard Saijou

Nicknamed "Leo." Part of Class
1-E, like Tatsuya. His father is half
Japanese and his mother a quarter.
Specializes in hardening magic.

"My brother should be returning soon..."

Miyuki Shiba

The younger sister of the Shiba siblings. Part of Class 1-A. An elite who entered Magic High as the top student. A Course 1 student, called a "Bloom," whose specialty is cooling magic. Her lovable only flaw is a severe brother complex.

Erika Chiba

Tatsuya's classmate. Has a bright personality; a troublemaker who gets everyone involved. Her family is large and famous for *kenjutsu*—a technique combining swords and magic.

"...Did you see?"

"I saw. I'm sorry."

"...Fine by me.
I'll teach you to
respect your
superiors."

Hanzou Gyoubu-Shoujou Hattori

A sophomore. The vice president of the student council.
His official school name is "Gyoubu Hattori." Takes pride
in being a Course 1 student, or a Bloom.

Azusa Nakajou

A sophomore.
Student council secretary.

Mari Watanabe

A senior.
Head of the disciplinary committee.

Suzune Ichihara

A senior.
Student council accountant.

"Vice President Hattori, would you like to have a mock duel with me?"

Mayumi Saegusa

A senior.
Student president of First High.

What are Magic High Schools?

A nickname for national high schools aimed at training modern magicians. There are nine schools placed throughout the country. Their locations are below.

1st High: Hachioji (Tokyo, Kanto)
2nd High: Nishinomiya (Hyogo, Kinki)
3rd High: Kanazawa (Ishikawa, Hokuriku)
4th High: Hamamatsu (Shizuoka, Tokai)
5th High: Sendai (Miyagi, Tohoku)

6th High: Izumo (Shimane, San'in)
7th High: Kochi (Kochi, Shikoku)
8th High: Otaru (Hokkaido)
9th High: Kumamoto (Kumamoto, Kyushu)

Of these, First High through Third High adopt a system of breaking two hundred incoming freshmen into Course 1 and Course 2 students (in Third High, these are called the Special Course and Normal Course). The difference between Course 1 and 2 students lies in whether they have teacher guidance. Aside from the fact that Course 2 students don't have access to personalized instruction, their curriculum is the same. Fourth High through Ninth High have one hundred students in their freshman class. Each of these receive personalized instruction, but they're considered to be a rank below First through Third High. The curriculum at each school follows a fundamental outline determined by the National Magic University, but certain schools do have unique features. For example, Third High places emphasis on practical magic for combat. In contrast, Fourth High focuses on magical engineering and significant, complex multi-process magic. Some offer prominent features not only in terms of magic but in terms of the environment one uses it in. For example, Seventh High teaches highly practical aquatic and water-based magic separately from the normal curriculum, whereas Eighth High includes outdoor training in magic effective at dealing with the harsh environmental conditions of tundra and high mountains.

The Irregular at Magic High School

ENROLLMENT PART I

1

Tsutomu Sato

Illustration **Kana Ishida**

YEN ON

NEW YORK

THE IRREGULAR AT MAGIC HIGH SCHOOL
TSUTOMU SATO

Translation by Andrew Prowse

© TSUTOMU SATO 2011
All rights reserved.
Edited by ASCII MEDIA WORKS
First published in Japan in 2011 by KADOKAWA CORPORATION, Tokyo.
English translation rights arranged with KADOKAWA CORPORATION, Tokyo,
through Tuttle-Mori Agency, Inc., Tokyo.

English translation © 2016 Hachette Book Group, Inc.

Yen On
Hachette Book Group
1290 Avenue of the Americas
New York, NY 10104

www.hachettebookgroup.com
www.yenpress.com

Yen On is an imprint of Hachette Book Group, Inc.
The Yen On name and logo are trademarks of Hachette Book Group, Inc.

The publisher is not responsible for websites (or their content) that are not owned by the publisher.

Library of Congress Cataloging-in-Publication Data

Names: Satou, Tsutomu. | Ishida, Kana, illustrator.
Title: The irregular at Magic High School. Volume 1, Enrollment. Part one /
   Tsutomu Satou ; Illustrations by Kana Ishida.
Other titles: Mahōka kōkō no rettosei. English | Enrollment
Description: First Yen On edition. | New York, NY : Yen On, 2016. | Originally published in Tokyo in 2011
   by Kadokawa Corporation under title: Mahōka kōkō no rettosei. | Summary: "The year is 2095. Magic
   has been tamed as another form of technology. Brother and sister Tatsuya and Miyuki Shiba are just
   about to start their first year at the renowned First Magic High School of Japan. But the school's ironclad
   rules mean that the brilliant Miyuki enters the prestigious Course 1, while her older brother, Tatsuya, is
   relegated to Course 2—and that's just the beginning of their troubles!"— Provided by publisher.
Identifiers: LCCN 2015042401 | ISBN 9780316348805 (paperback)
Subjects: | CYAC: Brothers and sisters—Fiction. | Magic—Fiction. | High schools—Fiction. |
   Schools—Fiction. | Japan—Fiction. | Science fiction.
Classification: LCC PZ7.1.S265 Ir 2016 | DDC [Fic]—dc23 LC record available at
   http://lccn.loc.gov/2015042401

10 9 8 7 6 5 4 3 2 1

RRD-C

Printed in the United States of America

The Irregular at MagicHigh School

ENROLLMENT
PART I

An irregular older brother with a certain flaw.
An honor roll younger sister who is perfectly flawless.

When the two siblings enrolled in Magic High School,
a dramatic life unfolded—

Glossary

Magic High School

A nickname for the high schools affiliated with the National Magic University. There are nine schools throughout the nation. Of them, First High through Third High each adopt a system of Course 1 and Course 2 students to split up its two hundred incoming freshmen.

Blooms, Weeds

Slang terms used at First High to display the gap between Course 1 and Course 2 students. Course 1 student uniforms feature an eight-petaled emblem embroidered on the left breast, but Course 2 student uniforms do not.

Course 1 student emblem

CAD (Casting Assistant Device)

A device that simplifies magic casting. Magical programming is recorded within. There are many types and forms, some specialized and others multipurpose.

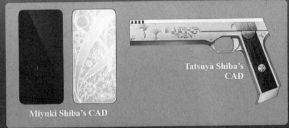

Tatsuya Shiba's CAD

Miyuki Shiba's CAD

Four Leaves Technology (FLT)

A domestic CAD manufacturer. Originally more famous for magic engineering products than for finished products, the development of the Silver model has made them much more widely known as a maker of CADs.

Taurus Silver

A genius engineer said to have advanced specialized CAD software by a decade in just a single year.

Eidos (individual information bodies)

Originally a term from Greek philosophy. In modern magic, *eidos* refers to the information bodies accompanying events. They are a record of those events existing in the world, and they can be called the footprints that events record upon the world. The definition of *magic* as it applies to its modern form is that of a technology that alters these events themselves by altering the eidos that make them up.

Idea (information body dimension)

Originally a term from Greek philosophy; pronounced "ee-dee-ah." In modern magic, *Idea* refers to the platform upon which eidos are recorded. Magic is primarily a technology that outputs a magic program onto the Idea and rewrites the eidos recorded there.

Activation program

The blueprints of magic, and the programming that constructs it. Activation programs are stored in a compressed format in CADs. The magician sends a psionic wave into the CAD, which then expands the data and uses it to convert the activation program into a signal, then returns it to the magician.

Psions (thought particles)

Massless particles belonging to the dimension of spirit phenomena. The information particles that record awareness and thought results. Eidos are considered the theoretical basis for modern magic, while activation programs and magic programs are the technology forming its practical basis—these are all bodies of information that are made up of psions.

Pushions (spirit particles)

Massless particles belonging to the dimension of spirit phenomena. Their existence has been confirmed, but their true form and function have yet to be elucidated. In general, magicians are only able to "sense" energized pushions.

Character

◆ **Honoka Mitsui**
Class 1-A. Miyuki's classmate.

◆ **Shizuku Kitayama**
Class 1-A. Miyuki's classmate.

◆ **Shun Morisaki**
Class 1-A. Miyuki's classmate.

◆ **Mayumi Saegusa**
A senior.
Student council president.

◆ **Hanzou Gyoubu-Shoujou Hattori**
A sophomore.
Student council vice president.

◆ **Suzune Ichihara**
A senior.
Student council accountant.

◆ **Azusa Nakajou**
A sophomore.
Student council secretary.

◆ **Mari Watanabe**
Chairwoman of the
disciplinary committee.

◆ **Koutarou Tatsumi**
A senior.
Member of the disciplinary committee.

◆ **Midori Sawaki**
A sophomore.
Member of the disciplinary committee.

◆ **Takeaki Kirihara**
A sophomore.
Member of the *kenjutsu* club. Junior High
Kanto *kenjutsu* tournament champion.

◆ **Sayaka Mibu**
A sophomore.
Member of the kendo club. Placed
second in the world at the girl's
junior high kendo tournament.

◆ **Katsuto Juumonji**
A senior.
Head of the club committee, the unified
organization overseeing all club activities.

◆ **Haruka Ono**
A general counselor of Class 1-E.

◆ **Yakumo Kokonoe**
A user of an ancient magic called *ninjutsu*.
Tatsuya's martial arts master.

Tatsuya Shiba

Class 1-E. A Course 2
(irregular) student, who are
mockingly called Weeds.

Miyuki Shiba

Class 1-A.
Tatsuya's younger sister;
enrolled as the top student.

Leonhard Saijou

Class 1-E.
Tatsuya's classmate.

Erika Chiba

Class 1-E.
Tatsuya's classmate.

Mizuki Shibata

Class 1-E.
Tatsuya's classmate.

[0]

Magic.

When did it become modern technology rather than a product of legend and fairy tale?

The first verifiable record of its use dates back to AD 1999.

An incident in which a police officer possessing special abilities stopped a nuclear terror attack by an extremist group trying to realize their prophecy of human extinction was the first confirmed example of magic in modern times.

At the time, the strange power was referred to as a supernatural ability. They believed that it was a purely inherent ability born out of a mutation and that the techniques couldn't be shared, spread, or systematized.

They were mistaken.

As research on supernatural abilities advanced, both in the East and West, more and more people appeared on the public stage to talk about "magic." Eventually, magic was able to reproduce those once supernatural powers.

Of course, one needed the talent. But it was the same as possessing skill in the arts or sciences—only those with a high predisposition could achieve professional levels of proficiency.

Supernatural abilities were systematized using magic, and magic became technology.

Those with supernatural abilities came to be called magic technicians.

These magic technicians were powerful enough to force even nuclear weapons to yield to them. To nations, they were both weapons and power itself.

At the end of the twenty-first century, in 2095, the nations of the world still have not shown signs of unification. They now compete with each other in the fostering of magic technicians.

The National Magic University Affiliated First High School.

It is known for being the most advanced institute of magical studies, which graduates the greatest number students to the National Magic University every year.

At the same time, it is an elite school that produces the greatest number of skilled magic technicians, who are known as "magicians."

There is no official stance of equal-opportunity magical education.

This country does not have the luxury of such indulgence.

And because of the glaring gap between those who can use magic and those who cannot, any kind of mediation is but an optimistic ideal.

Those who are out-and-out believers in talent.

Those who are almost cruel in their demand for actual skill.

That is the world of magic.

Simply being accepted into this school marks students as elite. And from the moment they enroll, there is already a difference between the honors students and the inferior.

Though they may all be equally new, they are not equal.

Even if they are brother and sister by blood.

[1]

"I won't stand for it."

"Are you still on about that…?"

It was early in the morning on the day of First High's entrance ceremony, but still two hours before it began.

The new students' hearts were all pounding with excitement over their new lives and the landscapes of their futures, but certainly few were as elated as these two.

In front of the auditorium, which would be the location of the entrance ceremony, a male and a female student, both clad in brand-new uniforms, were bickering.

Both were new students, yet their uniforms were slightly—but distinctly—different. It was not just the fact that the female uniform had a skirt and the male one had slacks. The emblem of First High, a design consisting of eight flower petals, was on the female student's chest. It wasn't on the male student's blazer.

"How could they make my brother an alternate? You had the top grades on the entrance exam! You should be the one representing the new students, not me!"

"Leaving aside the question of where you got my entrance exam grades from…this is Magic High School, so they obviously need to prioritize practical magic ability over the written test. You're well aware of my practical abilities, aren't you? I may have only reached Course 2, but I'm surprised I even got this far."

The female student was lashing out in harsh tones, and her male companion was currently trying to pacify her. Purely guessing from the female student calling him her brother, they might have been siblings—he the older, and she the younger. It wasn't impossible that they were closely related.

However, if they were brother and sister...

...then they were not very alike.

The younger sister was a cute girl who naturally drew stares. Ten out of ten people, even a hundred out of a hundred, wouldn't deny that she was lovely. The older brother, on the other hand, aside from his straightened back and sharp eyes, looked altogether average, without any features that stood out.

"Why can't you have more ambition than that? Nobody can beat you when it comes to studies and martial arts! I mean, even with magic, you're—"

The sister firmly berated the brother's weak-spirited statement, but...

"Miyuki!"

...he called her name in an even harsher tone of voice, causing Miyuki to catch her breath and close her mouth.

"We've been over this before. There's no point in talking about it."

"...I apologize."

"Miyuki..." He rested his hand on her bowed head. As he slowly caressed her glossy, smooth, long hair, the young man considered (rather pathetically) how to get her in a better mood. "...I *am* grateful you feel that way. You're always saving me by getting angry on my behalf," he said.

"You're lying."

"I'm not."

"Yes, you are. All you do is scold me..."

"I'm not lying! It's just that I feel about you the same way you feel about me."

"Oh, my… The same way…?"

…*What?* For some reason, the girl's cheeks flushed red.

He got the sense that there was some sort of disconnect he really shouldn't be ignoring. Nevertheless, he decided to shelve his doubts in order to resolve the problem at hand.

"Even if you refused to make the address, they would never choose me instead. You would lose face for sure if you were to refuse them at the last moment. And you actually know that, don't you? You're a smart kid, after all."

"That's—"

"Also, Miyuki… I'm looking forward to it. I'm proud to have you as my sister. Go out there and show your useless brother everything you have."

"You are not a useless brother, or anything of the sort! …But I understand. I apologize for my self-indulgence."

"There's nothing to apologize about, and I don't think it was self-indulgent at all."

"I'll be going, then. Make sure you watch."

"Yeah, you should go. I'll be looking forward to the main event."

The young woman bowed to excuse herself and disappeared into the auditorium. After seeing her off, the young man sighed to himself in relief.

So…what am I supposed to do now? He had accompanied the unwilling student representative to school for the rehearsal, but now he was at a loss, worrying about what to do for the two hours until the entrance ceremony began.

◇ ◇ ◇

The campus had three parts: a main building, a practicum building, and a laboratory building.

There was an auditorium/gymnasium whose inner layout was mechanically alterable. There were libraries on the third floor and the second basement floor. There were two smaller gymnasiums. There was a preparation building used for changing rooms, showers, storage, and club rooms. The dining hall / cafeteria / vending machine area was in another building, and there were various other structures both large and small filling First High's plot of land—it looked more like a suburban college campus than a high school.

The young man, in search of somewhere to sit while he waited for the entrance ceremony to begin, walked down a road of soft coat pavement made to resemble bricks as he looked back and forth.

The students used ID cards to gain access to the school's facilities, but those wouldn't be distributed to them until the ceremony ended. Even the public-facing café for visitors was closed today, perhaps to avoid the chaos.

After five minutes of walking around comparing what he saw to the map of the premises displayed on his portable terminal, he found a courtyard. It was behind the trees lining the path, which were positioned far enough apart not to obstruct the view.

Vaguely grateful it wasn't raining today, he sat down on a bench for three, then opened his portable terminal and accessed one of his favorite book websites.

This courtyard appeared to be a shortcut leading from the preparation building to the auditorium.

Perhaps *they* were being made to manage the ceremony—already-enrolled students (to him, upperclassmen) passed in front of him, leaving a little bit of space between them. On each of the students' left breasts was the eight-petaled emblem.

Their innocent malice scattered behind them as they walked away.

—Hey, isn't that kid a Weed?

—Here this early? …Pretty enthusiastic for a sub.

—He's just a spare, anyway.

A conversation he didn't want to hear drifted to his ears.

Weed was the term used to refer to Course 2 students.

Students with the eight petals on the left breasts of their green blazers were called Blooms from the emblem's design, and the students who didn't have them were called Weeds—since they wouldn't bloom into flowers.

This school had two hundred freshmen. Out of them, one hundred would be enrolled as students belonging to Course 2.

First High, an educational institution attached to the National Magic University, was a statutory body created to foster magic technicians. It was obligated to show a certain level of results in exchange for government funds. This school's quota—the number of students it was to supply to the National Magic University, an institution for advanced magical training—was at least one hundred.

Unfortunately, magic education was prone to accidents. Magic failures, whether in exercises or experiments, were directly correlated with accidents that were anything but minor. The students were aware of such dangers—they had staked their own futures on their magical talent and possibilities in striving to become magicians.

They had a rare talent, and when rare talents are highly valued by society, few can abandon them. That was all the more true when it came to emotionally immature young men and women. The only visions of their future left to them were the spectacular ones. That wasn't itself necessarily a bad thing, but the truth was that more than a few children would be hurt as a result of those ingrained values.

Thankfully, the accumulation of magical understanding had all but eliminated accidents resulting in death or physical handicaps.

But psychological factors could easily spoil magical talent. A significant number of students withdrew from school every year after trauma from an accident left them unable to use magic.

And the ones to make up for those losses were the Course 2 students.

They were permitted to register as students, attend classes, and make use of facilities and resources, but they had no access to the most important thing—individual magic practice with an instructor.

They studied unaided and produced results solely on their own merits. If they couldn't do that, they would only qualify themselves to graduate as general education students. Without being granted the right to graduate from a magic high school, they wouldn't be able to advance to the National Magic University.

Currently, the critical shortage of those who could teach magic forced them to prioritize those with talent. The Course 2 students were only allowed to enroll in the first place *under the premise that they would not be taught.*

It was officially prohibited to call Course 2 students Weeds. But it had established itself among even the Course 2 students themselves as a semipublic derogatory term. Even they thought of themselves as no more than spare parts.

That went for this young man as well. So there was no need to remind him of that fact by purposely speaking poorly of him within earshot. He had been fully aware of that much when he enrolled.

I really didn't ask for your opinion, he thought, directing his attention to the book data he'd downloaded to his information terminal.

◇ ◇ ◇

There was a clock displayed on his open terminal, and it pulled his reading-immersed mind back to reality.

Thirty minutes remained until the entrance ceremony.

"Are you a new student? It's opening time."

He logged out of his usual book website and closed his terminal, but as he was about to get up from the bench, a voice came down to him.

The first thing that caught his eye was the school uniform skirt. Then, the wide bracelet on her left wrist. It was the latest CAD model, but significantly thinner than the more common types, and with an eye toward fashion.

CAD—a Casting Assistant Device. It was also called simply a

device or an assistant. In this country, some used the term *broom*, which in addition to being a classic magic accessory, was also a shortening of the Japanese word for "magic operator."

It was an indispensable tool for modern magic technicians, providing activation programs for triggering magic in place of more traditional methods and tools such as incantations, charms, mudra, magic circles, and spell books.

Incantations to use magic properly with a single word or phrase hadn't been developed yet. Even when using methods in conjunction with one another, like charms and magic circles, actually reciting the spell would take anywhere from ten seconds to more than a minute depending on what it was. The CAD substituted all that for a simpler control scheme that let you do it in less than a second.

You could still perform magic without a CAD, but it had accelerated the casting process by leaps and bounds, to the point where there were virtually no magic technicians who didn't use one. Even the so-called espers, who could cause supernatural phenomena just by thinking about it, tended to sacrifice their specialization in certain areas in exchange for the speed and stability offered by the activation routine system.

However, not everyone could use magic just by having a CAD. They only provided the activation programs—actually executing the magic required the abilities of the magic technician himself. Therefore, CADs were useless to those who couldn't use magic. If you saw someone who had one, it was near certain that they were involved with magic.

And if Tatsuya recalled correctly, the only students permitted to carry their CADs around with them on school grounds were those on the student council and members of certain committees.

"Thank you. I'll be right over."

At her left breast was, of course, an eight-petaled emblem. The swell of her chest that pushed out her blazer didn't enter his mind.

He didn't bother to hide his own left breast. He wasn't so

servile—but that isn't to say he didn't feel a sense of inferiority. He had thought a student-council-worthy honors student wouldn't want to be so proactive in approaching him.

"I'm impressed. That's the kind with the screen, isn't it?"

But she apparently didn't share that opinion. She was smiling as though she were enjoying herself, looking at the film screen of the trifolding portable information terminal in his hands.

It was then that the young man saw her face at last. When he stood up from the bench, her head was about twenty centimeters below his. He was 175 centimeters tall, so even for a girl she was on the shorter side. She was at the perfect eye level to verify that he was a Course 2 student.

But there was absolutely no condescension in her eyes—only a pure, even innocent, admiration.

"Students are prohibited from carrying virtual display terminals inside our school. Unfortunately, that's the type most students use. But you've been using the kind with the screen even before you enrolled here, haven't you?"

"The virtual kind isn't suitable for reading, so..."

Anyone could tell at a glance that his terminal was something he was experienced with, so he didn't ask any unnecessary questions in return.

He had replied with what was almost an explanation, because he thought being too curt would end up disadvantaging his younger sister more than himself. She was the representative of the newly matriculated students, so there was no doubt she'd be chosen to the student council.

His calculated answer, however, only served to deepen this upperclassman's admiration.

"So you prefer reading to watching videos. You grow ever more unusual by the second. I appreciate printed materials more than images as well, so I'm rather happy to hear that."

They did live in an age where virtual materials were preferred to text, but book lovers were still far from exotic. She seemed possessed of an almost unusually sociable personality—even when her tone of voice and word choice were growing more informal by the second.

"Ah, I do apologize. I'm the student council president of First High, Mayumi Saegusa. It's written with the kanji for *seven* and *grass*. Pleased to meet you!"

She threw in a wink at the end, but her tone of voice was far from mysterious. With her gorgeous looks combined with her shapely body (despite her short stature), she had an alluring air that male students who had just entered high school couldn't help but misunderstand.

And yet, after hearing her introduce herself, he found himself wanting to scowl.

One of the Numbers…and Saegusa, at that?

Ability in magicians varied wildly based on genetic disposition. The family you're from was deeply important when it came to your merit as a magician. And in this country, it was customary for the families that possess exceptional blood for magic to have numbers in their surnames.

The Numbers were the lineages of magicians who had superior genetic predisposition, and the Saegusa family, with the character for *seven* in its name, was one of the two in Japan currently considered to be the most powerful. And this girl, who most likely was part of the direct bloodline, was this school's student council president.

In other words, she was an elite among elites. It might not be a stretch to say that they were polar opposites. He suppressed a bitter murmur at that, somehow managing a friendly smile as he introduced himself.

"I'm—ahem. My name is Tatsuya Shiba."

"Tatsuya Shiba… Ah, so you're *that* one…" Her eyes widened in a show of surprise. Then she nodded somewhat meaningfully.

Well, after all, she probably means "that" dropout who can barely use magic, despite being the older brother of the top new student, Miyuki Shiba. He chose to politely remain silent.

"Rumors about you are the talk of the teachers, you know." Mayumi giggled, not appearing to be bothered by Tatsuya's silence.

He figured the rumors were because of how different he and his younger sister were. Strangely enough, though, he didn't sense any of that sort of negative emotion from her. Her giggling held no nuance of scorn. Her smile only conveyed a positively friendly optimism.

"Your average across all seven subjects on the enrollment exam was 96 out of 100. The particular highlights were magical theory and magical engineering. The average score on those two subjects for those who passed didn't even come up to 70, and yet you scored perfectly on both, including the essay sections. They say that such a high score is unprecedented."

That sure sounded like frank praise, but Tatsuya decided he was only imagining it, because, after all—

"Those were my grades on the *written* test. They only go as far as the information system."

A Magic High School student's value was not based on his test grades but on his practical ability scores. Tatsuya indicated his left breast with a pained but friendly smile. There was no way the student council president wouldn't know what he meant by that.

But in response, Mayumi smiled and shook her head.

Not up and down—but left to right.

"At the very least, I wouldn't be able to emulate such amazing grades. I score fairly highly on theoretical subjects, too, but I don't think I could get the amazing score you did on the exam, even if I got the same questions as you!"

"Time is short, so... If you'll excuse me," Tatsuya told Mayumi, who still looked like she had things to say. He turned away from her without waiting for a reply.

Somewhere in his mind, he feared her smile, and feared her continuing to talk to him like this.

He wasn't sure why, though.

◇ ◇ ◇

Since Tatsuya had spent time talking to the student council president, more than half the seats in the auditorium were already filled by the time he entered.

The seating was not generally assigned—students were free to sit in the front row, the back row, right in the middle, on the sides, or wherever else they wanted.

Even in modern times, schools followed the old tradition of announcing who was in what class before the entrance ceremony, then seating the students by class. In this school, though, you wouldn't find out what class you were in until you were issued an ID card.

Therefore, the room didn't naturally split up by class.

There was, however, a clear rule governing the distribution of new students.

The front half was for the Blooms—the Course 1 students. The students with the eight-petaled emblem on their left breast. The new students who could enjoy the full curriculum the school had to offer.

The rear half was for the Weeds—the Course 2 students. The students with unadorned fabric on the pocket on their left breast. The new students who had been *allowed* to enroll and who would be treated as substitutes.

All the students may have been new freshmen starting school today, but they were evenly split between front and back based on the presence of that emblem—regardless of the fact that nobody was forcing them to do so.

Guess those who feel discrimination the strongest are those on the receiving end...

That was certainly a kind of wisdom to live by. He didn't feel like daring to go against it, so he found an empty seat near the middle in the back third of the room and sat down.

He glanced at the clock on the wall. Twenty minutes left.

Communications were restricted within the auditorium, so he

couldn't access his literature sites. He'd read through all the data saved to his terminal countless times anyway, and taking out his terminal in a place like this would be a breach of etiquette.

He tried to imagine his sister, who was probably going over her final rehearsal at the moment...and shook his head a little. There was no way she would be struggling right before the event.

In the end, without anything left to do, Tatsuya slid deeper into his cushionless chair and closed his eyes.

He was about to let himself fall asleep like that when somebody addressed him.

"Excuse me, is this seat open?"

He opened his eyes to check, and sure enough, it had been directed at him. As her voice had implied, it was a female student.

"Go ahead."

He was slightly dubious about why she would want to sit next to a male student she'd never seen before when there were plenty of other seats left. The seats themselves were fairly roomy, too, leaving aside how comfortable they were, and the girl in question had a narrow build (note: in terms of width, anyway, if not depth), so it wouldn't inconvenience Tatsuya at all if she were to sit next to him. In fact, it was a better deal than a sweaty ball of muscle staying there.

With that in mind, Tatsuya nodded amiably. The girl bowed her head, thanked him, and sat down. Three more girls came in one by one and sat next to her.

I see, thought Tatsuya, convinced. It seemed the four of them had been searching for a place where they could all sit together.

Are they friends? Seems unusual that four of them would all pass the exam to get into this difficult school, and that they'd all be Course 2 students, thought Tatsuya. He felt it wouldn't be as strange if at least one of them had better grades. —Though it didn't really matter to him.

He didn't have any further interest regarding his fellow freshmen who had coincidentally sat down next to him, so he redirected his gaze to the front. But then she addressed him once more.

"Excuse me..."

What could it be? She was clearly not someone he knew, and it wasn't that his elbows or feet were getting in her way. He didn't want to brag, but he had good posture. He didn't think he'd done anything to warrant objection. He crooked his head in confusion.

"My name is Mizuki Shibata. Pleased to meet you," came the unexpected self-introduction. Both her tone and appearance were timid. He knew you couldn't judge a book by its cover, but she didn't seem the type to appeal herself to others—so he decided she was probably forcing herself. *Maybe someone put a foolish idea in her head. Like Course 2 students needing to help each other out, since we already have a handicap, or something along those lines.*

"Tatsuya Shiba. Pleased to meet you too," he replied, with the softest attitude he could muster. A look of relief passed through her eyes behind her big lenses.

Girls wearing glasses were fairly unusual in this day and age.

As a result of the proliferation of orthoptic therapies starting around the mid-twenty-first century, the myopia condition was rapidly becoming a thing of the past. As long as you didn't have a fairly severe congenital abnormality in your eyesight, you didn't need vision-correcting tools. And if your eyesight did need correcting, contact lenses you could wear for years at a time without causing physical harm were also readily available.

Reasons to actually wear glasses came down to simple preference, fashion reasons, or...

...*pushion radiation sensitivity.*

Just by turning a bit, he could tell that her lenses weren't angled. At the very least, she wasn't wearing them to correct her vision. And from the impression he got, she probably didn't like them for their fashion value—he naturally thought she was wearing them out of some kind of need.

Pushion radiation sensitivity was a predisposition, a condition in which you saw too much. People with it could see pushion emissions without trying to, and they were unable to concentrate and make them go away. It was a type of perception control failure. But it wasn't an illness, nor was it an impediment.

The person's senses were just too sharp.

Pushions and psions...

Both were metapsychological phenomena—as was magic itself. They were observable particles that didn't fall under the category of fermions, particles constructed from matter, nor bosons, which created reciprocal action between matter. They were nonphysical particles. Current science believed that psions were particles that *gave form* to will and thought, while pushions *made up* the emotions created by will and thought.

Though unfortunately, that's all at the hypothetical stage.

Normally, psions were the particles utilized in magic, and modern magic's systematized techniques placed emphasis on controlling them. Magicians started out by learning psion manipulation techniques.

The light from pushion emissions affected the emotions of those who saw them. One theory said that was why pushions were the particles that made up emotions. Because of that, though, pushion radiation sensitivity tended to easily disrupt a person's mental balance.

The method of preventing this was, fundamentally, controlling one's sensitivity to pushions, but those who couldn't do so were assisted by an alternate, scientific means. One of those means was to wear glasses with special lenses called aura coating lenses.

Pushion radiation sensitivity actually wasn't an unusual condition for a magician to have. Sensitivity to pushions and sensitivity to psions were generally positively correlated, so it was thought that extreme sensitivity to pushion radiation was just something that many magicians—who consciously controlled psions—needed to deal with.

But symptoms of the level where one needed to block the pushion radiation with glasses at all times were indeed unusual. It would be one thing if she just had less than the normal ability to control them, but if it was because of an extremely strong sensitivity, then that would cause Tatsuya problems.

It's probably backward for her, though.

Tatsuya had been keeping a secret to himself.

A secret that, if witnessed normally, would be incomprehensible. He didn't need to worry about it being seen in the first place—but if she had special eyes that could perceive pushions and psions in the same way as visible light, she might notice it by sudden chance.

—He would probably need to act with more caution than normal when around her.

"I'm Erika Chiba. Nice to meet you, Shiba!"

"Same here."

His thoughts was interrupted by the voice of the girl sitting next to Mizuki.

But the interruption was also a well-timed relief. He had been staring at Mizuki unconsciously the whole time. She looked like she was about to burn out from shyness, but he hadn't realized it.

"But this is kind of a funny coincidence, isn't it?" Unlike her friend, this one didn't seem shy or scared around strangers. Her short hair, bright hair color, and handsome features amplified the impression of her being an energetic, lively person.

"What?"

"I mean, we have Shiba, Shibata, and Chiba, right? It's kind of like a pun, isn't it? I mean, not exactly, but still."

"...I see."

It certainly was not exactly a pun, but he understood what she was trying to say.

Even so, Chiba...*meaning "thousand leaves." Another one of the Numbers? I don't think there was a girl named Erika in* the *Chiba family, but it's possible she's part of a branch family...*

As he mused about it, the girls talked about how she was right, and how it was funny. Their laughter was somewhat out of place here, but it wasn't enough to draw any chilly stares.

After the two remaining girls across from Erika gave their introductions, Tatsuya found himself wanting to indulge his trivial curiosity. "Did the four of you go to the same junior high?"

Erika's answer, however, was unexpected. "No, we all just met a little while ago." She giggled, as though Tatsuya's expression of surprise was cute, and continued to explain. "I wasn't sure where to go, so I was having a staring contest with the directions board. Then Mizuki came up to me and we started talking."

"...The directions board?"

That's strange, though, thought Tatsuya. All of the information for the enrollment ceremony, including where it was to take place, had been distributed to every new student. If you used the LPS (local positioning system) that came standard on portable terminals, then even if you hadn't looked at the directions to the ceremony and even if you didn't remember *anything*, you wouldn't get lost.

"The three of us didn't bring our terminals, see..."

"Well, it says on the enrollment brochure that the virtual kind isn't allowed!"

"I barely made it in the first place, and I didn't want to have people staring at me already during the ceremony, you know?"

"I just happened to forget mine."

"So that's what happened..."

Honestly, though, he wasn't convinced. *This is your own entrance ceremony, so you could at least make sure you know where it is happening.* Those were his honest thoughts, but he didn't give voice to them.

No need to create meaningless discord, he thought prudently.

◇ ◇ ◇

Miyuki's address was, as predicted, fantastic. Tatsuya didn't have the faintest belief his sister would stumble over something as insignificant as this, though.

It had contained a handful of fairly risky phrases, like "everyone is equal," "united as one," "even outside magic," and "integral," but she wrapped them up well. He didn't feel so much as a hint of accusation in any of it.

Her attitude had been stately, but also fresh and modest. It went well with her uncommonly good looks, and she stole the hearts of all the boys there, freshmen and upperclassmen alike.

It would certainly be lively around her starting tomorrow.

But that, too, would be the same as always.

For one reason or another, Tatsuya's fondness of Miyuki was enough to be called a sister complex when compared to societal convention. He wanted to go congratulate her right away, but unfortunately, the postceremony time was used for distributing ID cards.

They hadn't created cards for everyone ahead of time. Instead, they would bring their normal identification there, and their school data would be written to a card on the spot. The process could be completed at any of the windows, but that, like the seating in the auditorium, created a natural wall.

Miyuki would probably—no, definitely—ignore that part, but as the representative of the incoming freshmen, she had already been conferred with a card anyway. And now there were tons of guests and student council members crowding around her.

"Shiba, what class are you in?" Erika asked him, unable to conceal her excitement. They had all moved to the windows as a group, with Tatsuya receiving his ID card last. (In other words, he was pretending to care about the "ladies first" thing.)

"Class E."

"Yes! We're in the same class!" She jumped for joy at his response. It was a bit of an exaggerated gesture, but...

"I'm in the same class, too." Mizuki looked excited, too, but she didn't make the same over-the-top movement. Maybe this was normal for new high school students.

"I'm in F class."

"I got G class, huh?"

But that wasn't to say that the light responses of the other two were any less enthusiastic. The important part was that they were in high spirits from this event—entering high school.

This school had eight classes per grade, and twenty-five students per class. And up until that point, it was equal.

But then, the Weeds, who weren't anticipated to bloom, were placed in classes E through H—separate from the "greenhouses" the Blooms would be placed in, since they were expected to blossom into huge flowers.

They naturally split up with the two female students who ended up in another class. They seemed to be going toward their respective homerooms. The homerooms were different just because they were split between A through D and E through H, but that didn't seem to put a damper on their excitement at all.

It wasn't as though every Course 2 student was hung up on it. There were plenty of kids who thought, *Wow, I managed to get into an elite school that was a little out of my reach*, too. The school was rated as one of the top in the country even for subjects other than magic, after all. The two of them had probably gone looking for friends in their classes that they'd be spending the next year with.

"What do you want to do? Should we drop by our classroom, too?" asked Erika, looking up at Tatsuya's face. Mizuki didn't ask, probably because she was also looking up at him.

Aside from schools that preserved old traditions, high schools didn't use homeroom teachers these days. They didn't need people to call students to the office—and the luxury of wasting personnel expenses on something like that was rare. Everything was handled by communications among terminals connected to the school network.

The norm for decades now had been to give each student a personal terminal to use in school. These information terminals were even used for personal teaching, as long as it wasn't for skill coaching or other large-scale activities. If a student needed further care, schools always had multiple professionally qualified counselors of many different fields of expertise on staff.

The reason, then, that homeroom itself was necessary was because it was convenient for practice and experiments. They needed to preserve a certain number of people so practice and labs would end both on time and without any extra time. *Though leftovers still spring up every day...* Plus, having your own assigned terminal was also highly convenient for many reasons.

It didn't matter what the scenery was like—spending a long time in a single room meant that you would naturally deepen exchanges with others. The removal of homeroom teachers actually tended to strengthen relationships between students.

In any case, going to homeroom would be the quickest option if they wanted to make new friends. Tatsuya, however, shook his head at Erika's request.

"Sorry. I'm supposed to meet up with my younger sister."

He knew there would be no classes or announcements today. He had promised Miyuki to return home with her right after he'd finished up with her formalities.

"Wow... She must be pretty cute if she's your sister, Shiba, huh?" murmured Erika. It sounded like both an impression and a question, and left him without quite knowing how to answer her. *What does she mean by "if she's your sister"?* he thought. He felt like her conclusion wasn't following from her logic.

Fortunately, there was no reason to force himself to answer, because Mizuki asked him a more fundamental question. "A younger sister... Could she be Miyuki Shiba, the new student representative?"

This time, he didn't need to worry. He answered the question with a single nod to strongly imply affirmation.

"Wait, really? Are you twins?" asked Erika.

It was understandable question, and one Tatsuya was pretty used to. "We get asked that a lot, but we're not twins. I was born in April, and she was born in March. If I had been born a month earlier, or my sister a month later, we wouldn't have been in the same grade."

"Huh... That sounds kind of complicated."

It was certainly complicated being in the same grade as his younger sister—an honors student—but Erika didn't mean any harm by the question.

Tatsuya smiled and passed over it. "But I'm surprised you figured it out. Shiba isn't that unusual a last name."

The two girls smiled a little at his response. There was a notable difference in shade between them, though.

"No, no, it's pretty unusual!" Erika smiled painfully.

"Your faces look alike..." Mizuki, though, smiled in a reserved, insecure way for some reason.

"Do they?" Tatsuya couldn't help but be a little confused. It probably indicated that Mizuki's words came from the same foundation as Erika's, but he just didn't feel it was true.

Or rather, he couldn't believe it.

Even if he removed himself from the favorable light he cast on her as a family member, Miyuki was an uncommonly pretty girl. Even without her exorbitant abilities, she couldn't help but attract attention wherever she went. She was a natural-born idol—no, a star.

When he looked at her, he was always reminded of the proverb that God never grants gifts to a person—and how much of a lie *that* was.

Tatsuya's own measurement of self-worth was, upon reflection, a bit above average, or maybe in the upper-middle zone.

During junior high, he would see his sister getting love letters practically on a daily basis (though Tatsuya saw them more as fan mail than anything else). He'd never received anything like that even once, though. They *should* share the same genetic code—well, some of it, anyway—but that didn't stop Tatsuya from doubting their blood relationship time and time again.

However, Erika nodded readily at Tatsuya's response—or rather what Mizuki had said. "Now that you mention it... Yeah, they do look alike! I mean, Shiba is a cutie himself. And it's not just how his face looks. It's like, the kind of air around him, or something."

"A cutie? How many decades ago did that term go out of style...? Besides, if you disregard our faces, we don't look anything alike, do we?"

What Erika had said was probably unintuitive and a little difficult to understand, but apparently she wasn't trying to say their faces were similar. That was how Tatsuya translated it, at least, which was why he couldn't help but make that retort.

"That's not it. It's like... How do I put it...?" Erika didn't seem to be able to express it well herself. She might have stood there groaning for a while had Mizuki not come to her rescue.

"It's your aura. It makes your expressions seem really dignified. It's what I would expect from siblings."

"That's it! Your auras!" Erika's head bobbed up and down vigorously and she nearly slapped her knees.

Now it was Tatsuya's turn to give her a dry smile. "Chiba... You're actually kind of a clown, you know?"

"A clown?" In typical fashion, he only half-listened to her cry of "How rude!" From her tone of voice, Erika didn't sound like she was very bothered by it, either.

"Still, Shibata, you're good at reading the auras in people's expressions... You really have good eyes." Those words, on the other hand, were spoken meaningfully.

"Huh? But Mizuki wears glasses," wondered Erika aloud.

"That's not what I mean. Besides, her lenses aren't curved at all, are they?"

Confused, Erika peered into Mizuki's glasses. On the other side of her lenses, her eyes had frozen in surprise.

Was she surprised someone had noticed it, or disappointed that she hadn't hidden it? Whichever the case was, Tatsuya didn't think it was as big a deal as she was making it out to be.

He didn't have a chance to investigate why she was making that kind of face, though. He was out of time, and that was probably the only reason the conversation ended on a good note.

◇ ◇ ◇

"I'm sorry I made you wait, Tatsuya."

As Tatsuya and the others conversed in a corner near the auditorium exit, he heard the voice of the one he was waiting for from behind them.

Miyuki had broken out of the crowd surrounding her.

That was quick was his first thought, but he corrected himself—considering her temperament, it was probably the right time.

She was far from nonsocial, but her fussiness toward flattery and niceties couldn't be denied. It wasn't quite childlike, but she'd certainly never been spared any praise when she was young. In return, though, she had plenty of the superficial kind, mixed with envy and gossip.

Thinking from that perspective, she would have naturally gotten quite used to being fawned over. He would say that she'd actually endured quite a bit today.

He'd planned to turn around and remark, "That was fast," and while he managed to speak the words, his intonation ended up being rather interrogative, because there was someone with Miyuki he hadn't expected to see.

"Hello, Shiba. We meet again."

Tatsuya silently bowed to her amiable smile; her words seemed to be trying to patch things up with him. Despite his response lacking friendliness, the student council president, Mayumi Saegusa, didn't break her smile. Perhaps that was her poker face, or maybe she was just comfortable in her own territory. Tatsuya had just met her, so he couldn't tell one way or the other.

But his sister seemed to be more interested in the girls cozying up next to him (?) than in his odd reply to the student council president.

"Tatsuya, who are these people...?"

Before explaining why she wasn't by herself, she asked Tatsuya to explain why he wasn't by *him*self. It felt a little abrupt, but there was no reason to hide it. He answered without skipping a beat. "This is Mizuki Shibata. And this is Erika Chiba. We're in the same class."

"I see... On a date with your classmates already?" she asked, making a cute face and tilting her head. Her expression said *And I certainly don't mean anything by that*. A ladylike smile was on her lips—but her eyes weren't smiling.

Oh my, thought Tatsuya. She'd been under concentrated fire from the grating flattery ever since the ceremony ended, and it seemed like she'd accumulated quite a bit of stress.

"Of course not, Miyuki... I was just talking to them while waiting for you. Saying that was rude to them, you know."

Personally, he thought her sulking face was cute, too, but not naming yourself when introduced to someone wouldn't look good in front of the upperclassmen and other new students. Tatsuya let a twinge of criticism creep into his eyes. Miyuki looked surprised, then gave a much more graceful smile.

"Pleased to meet you, Miss Shibata, Miss Chiba. I am Miyuki Shiba. I am a new student here as well, so I look forward to getting along with you as my brother is."

"I'm Mizuki Shibata. Pleased to meet you as well."

"Nice to meetcha. You can just call me Erika. Would it be okay for me to just call you Miyuki, too?"

"Yes, go right ahead. Using my last name would make it hard to distinguish between my brother and me, after all."

The three girls exchanged introductions again.

Miyuki and Mizuki's introduction was appropriate for a first meeting. But Erika, on the other hand, was already acting very friendly to her (to put it nicely). However, Tatsuya was the one who found himself hesitating at her friendly language. Miyuki instead

nodded, not showing a hint of dislike for her familiar tone and slightly more affable attitude.

"Ah-ha, Miyuki, you actually seem easy to get along with, despite how you look!"

"And you have a very open personality, just as you look. Nice to meet you, Erika."

Miyuki, who was sick of all the flattery and niceties, probably appreciated Erika's candid attitude more than she might have otherwise. There did seem to be something more than that being communicated between them, though. They exchanged frank, unreserved smiles.

Tatsuya couldn't help but feel left out, but they couldn't just keep standing here. They were with the student council president's party that came with his sister, so they wouldn't be seen as nuisances, but doing this for much longer would make them into a traffic obstruction.

"Miyuki. Did you finish up with the student council? If you're not, then maybe we shouldn't be standing around."

"It's all right." Someone else answered his question and proposition. "We were just meeting each other today. Miyuki—may I also call you that?" addressed Mayumi.

"Oh, yes." Miyuki changed her candid smile into a docile expression and nodded.

"Then, Miyuki, we will discuss further details another day."

Mayumi gave a slight bow with a smile and went to leave the auditorium. But the male student who had been waiting right behind her called out to her. On his chest, just as expected, was the eight-petaled emblem.

"But, President, our plans—"

"We did not promise anything beforehand. If she has her own plans, we should prioritize that, right?"

Controlling the male student, who showed signs of not backing down, with her eyes, Mayumi turned a meaningful smile on Miyuki and Tatsuya.

"Then I will take my leave, Miyuki. Shiba—another time, I hope."

Mayumi bowed a second time and left. The male student following her turned around and glared at Tatsuya with an expression that was none too friendly.

◇ ◇ ◇

"...Should we go home, then?"

Right off the bat, he seemed to have fallen out of an upperclassman's grace, and one who was a student council member at that. But it had been almost inevitable. His life had never gone so smoothly and easily that he'd need to worry over something like this. That life hadn't lasted even sixteen years yet, but he had plenty of experience with such negativity.

"I'm sorry, Tatsuya. I gave them a bad impression of you—" Miyuki started, her expression clouded.

"It's nothing for you to apologize about," Tatsuya interrupted her sentence, shaking his head and putting his hand on her head. He stroked her hair as though his hand were a comb, and her sullen expression changed to one tinged with intoxication. Those watching them couldn't deny that they were acting questionably for siblings, but neither Mizuki nor Erika said anything about it, perhaps out of restraint since this was their first meeting.

"Since we're here, why not go have some tea?"

"That sounds great! I'm in! Apparently there's a delicious cake shop around here."

Instead, the girls tossed them an invitation to a tea party.

Tatsuya didn't intend to ask if their families would get worried— even mentioning something like that would be needless consideration. And in this regard, Tatsuya and Miyuki were the same.

Above all, Tatsuya had something he wanted to ask. It was something that was honestly no big deal, but it had been bothering him to the point where he couldn't let it go.

"You didn't check where the entrance ceremony was going to be, but you know where a cake shop is?"

Maybe the question was a little mean, but Erika nodded confidently, without a shred of hesitation. "Of course! Isn't it important?"

"Of course..." he repeated. His words came out as a groan, but he didn't care who got mad at him for it.

But it seemed like he was the only one shocked by Erika's "outburst."

"Tatsuya, what shall we do?" Miyuki wasn't acting as though she cared at all about Erika's senseless prioritization of the location of a sweets shop over that of the ceremony venue. —Of course, Miyuki didn't know how that came about in the first place.

However, he didn't have to think too hard about agreeing with them. "Why not? You made acquaintances, you know? You can't have too many friends of the same gender and grade level." There was no particular reason they had to hurry back home. Tatsuya had originally planned to spend the afternoon somewhere to celebrate *his sister* enrolling, anyway.

The fact that he hadn't thought very deeply about what he said let his truly unconcerned feelings about it come to the surface.

Erika and Mizuki also understood what he really thought of it, which was probably why they responded how they did.

"When it comes to Miyuki, Shiba leaves himself out, huh..."

"He's very considerate toward his sister..."

Their stares each had its own mixture of praise and bewilderment. Tatsuya could only come back with a silent, uncomfortable smile.

◇ ◇ ◇

The "cake shop" that Erika brought them too had actually been a French-style cafeteria with good desserts, so they ate lunch there and made merry with long conversation (though since there were three girls present, Tatsuya mostly just listened). Evening was already upon them when they got back home.

No one came out to greet them.

Tatsuya and Miyuki lived mostly by themselves in this house, which was much larger than the average home.

He went to his room and took off his uniform first.

They seemed to have gone to great lengths to make the difference stand out on his blazer. He didn't want to believe that something so silly was affecting him emotionally, but when he took it off, he did feel his mood improve a bit. He scoffed at his own feelings, then quickly finished getting change.

Shortly afterward, as he was unwinding in the living room, Miyuki came downstairs. She had changed into her house clothes. Though materials engineering had advanced by leaps and bounds, clothing designs hadn't changed much since a hundred years ago. The fetching lines of her legs stretched from her short skirt, which was reminiscent of early twenty-first-century styles.

For whatever reason, his sister's sense of fashion featured more exposure when in the house. He should have gotten used to it by now, but lately she had gotten a lot more girly, and Tatsuya frequently found himself unsure of where to look.

"Tatsuya, shall I get you something to drink?"

"Hmm. I'll have coffee, thanks."

"I will be right back."

Her hair, loosely tied in a single clump, swayed across her slim back as she moved toward the kitchen. She tied it back so it wouldn't get in the way when she was working in the kitchen. Because of that, though, the white nape of her neck, normally hidden behind her long hair, was going in and out of sight because of her sweater with a wide neckline, producing an indescribable allure.

In developed nations, where the use of a home automation robot (HAR, or "Haru" for short) was widespread, women standing in the kitchen—and men, too, of course—were becoming something of a rarity. Full-fledged cooking was one thing, but only those who were interested did minor things like make toast or coffee on their own.

And Miyuki belonged to that rare group of people.

She didn't particularly have any mechanical ineptitude. Whenever friends came over, she mostly left it to their HAR. But when it was just the two of them, she never spared the trouble.

The crunching sound of the beans being ground and the bubbly sound of the hot water boiling tickled Tatsuya's ears. It was the simplest of paper drip bags, but the fact that she wouldn't even use an older coffeemaker meant that it must have been some kind of fixation.

He had asked her about it once, and she'd answered, "Because I like it," so it was probably something like a hobby. When he asked if it was, he remembered her giving him a sullen look, though.

Whatever the case, the coffee Miyuki made matched his palate the best.

"Here you are, Tatsuya."

She placed the cup on the side table, then went around to the other side and sat down next to him. The coffee she had put on the table was black, and the coffee in the cup in her hand had milk in it.

"It's good."

There was no need to eulogize it. Miyuki smiled, happy with just those two words.

She watched her brother take a second sip, his face satisfied. Then, with an expression of relief, she put her own cup to her mouth. That was what she always did.

The two of them enjoyed their coffee like that for a while.

Neither of them tried to force conversation.

They didn't care that they had someone to talk to right next to them.

It had been an extremely long time since the two of them felt awkward at long periods of silence between them.

There were plenty of things to talk about. Today was the entrance ceremony. They had made new friends, and a somewhat concerning upperclassman had appeared. Miyuki had, as expected, been invited to join the student council. They could be up all night recalling the day's events and talking about them.

But the siblings sat next to each other in their house, alone, silently sipping their coffee.

"—I'll go get dinner started."

Miyuki stood up with her now-empty cup. Tatsuya gave his cup of coffee to her outstretched hand and got up as well.

Night fell on the siblings, the same as it always did.

[2]

He awoke on the second day of high school in the same way as the first. He may have advanced to high school, but it wasn't as though the earth's rotational period had changed.

He splashed a bit of water on his face—he would clean it more thoroughly again later—and changed into his usual outfit.

When he went down into the dining room, he found that Miyuki had already started making breakfast.

"Good morning, Miyuki. You're up earlier than usual today."

Dawn was just breaking, and the spring sun had yet to show its face.

It was still far too early to go to school, of course. School started at eight o'clock sharp, and it took them thirty minutes to get to school, including walking. They just needed to leave at 7:30. Making breakfast, eating it, and cleaning up... Even all that would end up leaving them with more than an hour of free time.

"Good morning, Tatsuya." She held out a cup with fresh juice in it. "Here you go."

"Thank you." After politely thanking her, he downed it in one gulp and placed it back into her outstretched hand. —Miyuki had a perfect grasp of how long it took Tatsuya to breathe.

As she turned back toward the kitchen counter, he was about to tell her he'd return shortly, but Miyuki suddenly stopped working and turned to him again.

"Tatsuya, I was thinking that perhaps I could go with you this morning..."

As she finished her sentence, she held up a basket containing sandwiches to him. She hadn't started making breakfast a minute ago—she must have actually just finished it.

"I don't mind, but... In your uniform?" Tatsuya asked, glancing between the sweats he was wearing to the school uniform that appeared from underneath her apron.

"I still haven't reported my promotion to Sensei, so... And besides, I can no longer keep up with your training," answered Miyuki.

So she had changed into her uniform this early so that she could go show it off to the man. "All right. You don't need to do the same thing for training as I do, but if that's the case, I'm sure Master will be happy... I just hope he's not so happy he loses his self-control."

"Just protect me if that happens, okay?"

His sister cutely shut one eye, and a natural smile crossed Tatsuya's face.

◇ ◇ ◇

The brisk, early-morning air was still chilly as she *hovered up* the sloping road, her long hair and skirt hem fluttering in the breeze.

Miyuki was dashing up the long, gentle mountain road without kicking off at all in defiance of the laws of gravity. She was pushing sixty kilometers per hour.

Tatsuya ran beside her. He, though, was jogging—but his stride was more than ten meters long. Compared to Miyuki, however, his expression was in no way relaxed.

"Shall I slow my pace a bit...?" asked Miyuki, swiveling around and sliding up backward on one foot.

"No—it wouldn't be training then," answered Tatsuya, not out of breath, but clearly growing fatigued.

Their shoes didn't have some kind of propulsion mechanism inside or anything—needless to say, their speed was a product of magic.

Miyuki was using magic to slow the gravitational acceleration being applied to her, as well as magic to move her own body toward a destination up the slope.

Tatsuya was using magic to amplify the acceleration and deceleration created by kicking off the road, as well as magic to suppress his movement in the vertical direction so he wouldn't launch himself off the ground.

Both were simple compound techniques to control movement and acceleration. Miyuki was one thing, but because of their simplicity even Tatsuya, who was only able to become a Course 2 student, was able to continuously cast it.

In this case, it was difficult to say for sure who had it harder—Miyuki in her in-line skates, or Tatsuya running under his own power.

At a glance, Miyuki looked like she had it easier, since her in-line skates were lessening her physical exertion. Since she wasn't using her own feet, though, she needed to use magic to control her movement vector in *every* direction. Tatsuya, on the other hand, was determining his direction of movement by actually running.

Tatsuya needed to keep casting the spell with every step, while Miyuki couldn't take her hands off the spell's controls for even a moment.

The two had each assigned themselves fundamentally different exercise regimens.

◇ ◇ ◇

Their destination was about ten minutes from their house—well, at the speed at which they were running—and sitting atop a small hill.

In a word, it was a temple. But those who gathered there seemed like a far cry from priests, monks, or novices. If you needed a good term for them, they were pretty close to warrior monks.

Girls, and especially young girls, would normally be too scared to come near the temple's atmosphere. Miyuki, though, passed right on through it without hesitation on her in-line skates. It was strange to see her being so bold, since she was so well mannered all the time. The owner, however, had said "I don't mind" so many times it had started to get annoying, so everyone was already used to it.

Tatsuya wasn't there, but not because he couldn't keep pace with Miyuki. He was in the middle of a violent welcome that burst on him as soon as he entered the temple gate.

This *welcome* was essentially just practice, though.

When he first started coming to this temple, he would practice against one senior member at a time. At this point, though, instead of such a round-robin format, they would just throw twenty beginner pupils at him all at once.

Miyuki stopped in the front garden of the main temple, worried, and turned back toward her brother, who was now buried in the crowd. She heard a bright voice from behind her.

"Ah, Miyuki! It's been quite a while."

Her senses were very sharp, so she had been suitably cautious about the experience repeating itself—but because of that, it shocked her even more. She slowly came to realize the futility of it, but she still couldn't help but protest. "Sensei…I have asked you many times over not to conceal yourself and sneak up on me…"

"Don't sneak up on you? You make some pretty tough requests yourself, Miyuki. I'm a *shinobi*, after all. Sneaking up on people is our nature."

With his neatly trimmed hair and *yukata* dyed in black, the man looked appropriate for the situation. His *actual* age aside, his looks and the air he gave off were anything but old.

He was just wandering about, but he exuded a vulgarity that was difficult to describe. And though he wore priestly clothing, he was indescribably suspicious.

"You can't get employed as a ninja anymore. I wish you would reform that nature of yours."

But even Miyuki's serious protest was answered by a tongue clicking and hand waving. "Tsk, tsk, tsk. I'm no ninja—they're snobs, and riddled with misunderstandings—I'm a historically accurate *shinobi*. It's not an occupation, it's a tradition!"

—He was, in any case, vulgar.

"I'm aware that you are historically accurate. That's why I find it strange. Sensei, why are you so—" —*frivolous*? Miyuki didn't say the word. She had already learned it would do her no good.

This fake priest—well, on paper, he *was* a real priest—was named Yakumo Kokonoe, and he was a self-styled *shinobi*, the more general term for which was "*ninjutsu* user."

As he himself was insisting, he passed down old forms of magic. He was clearly different from the premodern spies who excelled only in physical abilities.

Magic was an object of science. When the masses fully realized that it was more than pure fiction, people learned that *ninjutsu*, too, was no mere classical martial art and system of spy techniques—the truly secret parts were a variety of magic.

The uncanny techniques that had been thought to be false—*made* to be thought of as false—were actually closer to the true form of *ninjutsu*.

Of course, as was the case with other magical systems, not everything in legends was truth.

They discovered that their "transformations," essentially the classic storybook example of *ninjutsu*, were simply combinations of illusions and high-speed movement. Shadow cloning techniques—and not just those from *ninjutsu*, but from traditional magic in general—were varieties of this trick. Actual cloning, transformation, and transmutation were all fields defined as impossible by modern magic.

Yakumo Kokonoe, whom Miyuki called Sensei and Tatsuya called Master, was a successor of the old magic, the true art of *ninjutsu* passed down for a very long time.

But even leaving aside his priestly attire (which also seemed con-trived), his own appearance and behavior both seemed quite far away from *historically accurate*...

"Is that the First High uniform?"

"Yes, yesterday was the entrance ceremony."

"I see, I see! Hmm, yes, very nice."

"...I thought I would, um, tell you I started school..."

"Such a fresh, brand-new uniform. So clean and tidy, and yet it has this irresistible allure."

"..."

"It is like a flower bud about to bloom—a newborn, tender sprout blossoming forth. Yes...it is *moé*! This is *moé*! Hm?"

He went on and on, getting more excited, and kept inch-ing toward Miyuki as she edged backward. But then, suddenly, he whipped around, squatted, and raised his left hand above his head.

There was a *smack* as his arm blocked a downward chop.

"Master, you're scaring Miyuki. Could you calm down a little?"

"...Not bad, Tatsuya. You took me by...*surprise!*"

Keeping Tatsuya's right hand busy with his left, Yakumo fired a right straight at him.

Tatsuya broke the joint lock by waving his right hand up, then back down, and then took the attack as if wrapping it up, then grabbed on to Yakumo's side.

He didn't fight it—he rolled forward, and his foot flew toward the back of Tatsuya's head. Tatsuya quickly dodged it with a twist.

The two came apart.

There was an audible exhalation from the spectators.

A ring had formed around their face-off at some point.

Tatsuya and Yakumo went in again.

Miyuki wasn't the only one whose hands were sweating.

◇ ◇ ◇

This customary, every-morning disturbance had been continuing ever since Tatsuya was a freshman in junior high—that October, to be precise. After it ended, the temple grounds were once again quiet. The novices all returned to their religious services, leaving the Shiba siblings and Yakumo alone in the front yard of the main temple.

"Here you are, Sensei. Tatsuya, would you like some as well?"

"Oh, Miyuki, thank you!"

"...Give me a moment."

Yakumo smiled and took a towel and a cup from Miyuki. His expression still seemed relaxed, despite his sweating. Tatsuya, on the other hand, was sprawled out on the ground trying to bring his violent breathing back under control. After raising a hand and replying to Miyuki, he managed to peel himself off the ground.

"Tatsuya, are you all right...?"

He had sat up, but he was still on the ground. Miyuki knelt down next to him, worried, not being careful to not get her skirt dirty, and used the towel in her hand to wipe his dripping sweat.

"I'm fine." Yakumo's disagreeably warm stare wasn't particularly bothering him, but Tatsuya pulled the towel from Miyuki's hand, and with a deep breath, he rallied his energy and stood up.

"Sorry for getting dirt on your skirt." Tatsuya's own sweats were a bit more than a little dirty, but Miyuki offered no words to point it out.

"This much is no problem at all," answered Miyuki with a smile. Instead of brushing off her skirt hem, she removed a long, thin portable terminal from her inside pocket. Then she fluidly typed a short number into the force feedback panel covering most of its surface.

The CAD that Miyuki owned was a multipurpose one made in the shape of a portable terminal. It was more risky to have than the most popular multipurpose CAD, which was made in the shape of a bracelet. However, the advantage to getting used to one was that you could use it with one hand. It was the preferred model of higher-ranking magicians who did lots of field work, since they disliked both hands being occupied.

The nonphysical light drew a complex pattern in her right hand, which was then absorbed into the CAD, and then the magic activated.

Modern magicians used a CAD—an electronic device born of magical engineering—in place of staffs, grimoires, incantations, mudra, and the like.

CADs came loaded with a synthetic substance called a Reaction Stone that converted psionic signals to electrical ones and vice versa. It used the psions supplied by the magician to activate an electronically recorded magic circle, or activation program.

Activation programs were the blueprints for magic. Each program contained at least the same amount of information as tedious incantations, complex symbols, and hastily assembled seal arrangements.

Human flesh was a good conductor of psions, so when the CAD emitted the activation program, the magician would absorb it through their skin. Then it would be sent to their magic calculation region, a subconscious mental system that magicians possessed. This region of the brain would then construct a magic program—a body of information that would implement the magic—using the activation program as a base.

In this way, a CAD instantly supplied all the information required to construct magic.

From out of nowhere, an intangible cloud appeared and wrapped itself around Miyuki. It started at her skirt, then crawled down her black leggings all the way to the tips of her boots, which she'd removed the in-line skate attachments from.

In addition, a few particles bubbling forth from midair drifted to Tatsuya's back, then floated down his whole body.

Once the thin, faintly shining mist cleared, she was wearing an immaculate uniform, and his gym clothes were absolutely spotless.

"Would you like breakfast, Tatsuya? Sensei, you can eat with us if you like," Miyuki said in a completely normal tone of voice. She lightly held up her basket, as if it had been the most natural thing in the world.

Tatsuya was actually well aware that this level of magic was practically nothing for his little sister.

◇ ◇ ◇

Once they all sat down on the balcony, Tatsuya and Yakumo began filling their mouths with the sandwiches. Miyuki was taking only one bite at a time, since she was waiting on Tatsuya hand and foot, offering him tea and exchanging his dishes for him.

Yakumo watched them with a warm, yet somehow obnoxious expression. He took a towel that one of his monk pupils (complete with shaved head) held out for him and used it to clean his hands and mouth. Finally, he put his hands together and thanked Miyuki for the food, and murmured in a somewhat quiet and serious tone, "I may not be able to match up with Tatsuya in terms of raw physical ability anymore..."

Those were unmistakably words of praise. If the other novices had been here, they would have showered Tatsuya in unavoidable stares of envy—and the pupil waiting beside Yakumo *was* actually gazing at him with a mixture of resentment and jealousy.

Miyuki's face was shining as if his praise had been directed at her. But Tatsuya's mind couldn't accept that simple commendation at face value.

"We have the same physical abilities, yet you're still pulverizing me with one hand tied behind your back... And I'm supposed to be happy?" said Tatsuya. It was as much a rebuttal as it was a complaint.

Yakumo gave a tired smile. "It's what we call *only natural*, Tatsuya. I am your master, and we sparred in my personal ring. You're still fifteen. My students would all run away if I fell behind a child like you!"

"I think you should be a little more honest, Tatsuya. It isn't every day that Sensei gives you a compliment. I think you should stick out your chest and smile about it."

Both Yakumo and Miyuki spoke with teasing tones, but Tatsuya wasn't so dense that he failed to grasp the admonishment from the former and the encouragement from the latter.

His bitter grin lost its bitterness and turned into a plain old grin.

"...I'd still look pretty bad if I did that..."

◇ ◇ ◇

The people on their way to work or school boarded the small, stationary train cars one by one in an orderly fashion.

The term *full train* was basically extinct.

Trains had remained the main form of public transportation, but these hundred years had changed the idea behind it. Nobody used the large train cars that could hold dozens of people anymore, save for the few long-distance, high-speed trains where one's seat needed to be reserved.

Instead, two-person cars called cabinets—small, linear, and government regulated—had become the modern norm. The tracks supplied them with both propulsion and energy, so they were about half as big as an automobile meant for the same number of people.

People were boarding the cabinets lined up on the platform in order, starting with the lead one. Once inside, they scanned in their destinations using tickets and passes, and the cabinets proceeded onto the service tracks.

Train lines were split into three tracks according to speed. An automatic traffic system controlled the distances between cars. It would also move you up the tracks from low speed to high speed. Then, as you approached your destination, it would shift you back down to the low-speed rails and deliver you to the platform. The system was similar to how cars change lanes on highways, but it was highly efficient due to advances in artificial neural networks, securing the same throughput as dozens of larger cars linked together.

In the case of mid- or long-distance intracity travel, your cabinet would be loaded onto a trailer, which would run on a fourth, faster track. Passengers would then be able to exit their cabinet, use the trailer's facilities, and relax, but they weren't used for commuting that often.

Coincidental meetings on trains, like the kind in old romance novels, never occurred with this modern train system. But in exchange for not being able to meet up with friends on the train ride, you wouldn't need to fear the risk of molestation.

There were no security cameras or microphones within the cabinets. Because they were made so you couldn't leave them while they were running, seats were equipped with emergency dividers between them. More important, the consensus of society was that passengers' privacy was of utmost importance. Trains had become a private space, just like personal cars.

The cabinets, equipped with measures to prevent more than one person boarding at the same time, worked on a system where you'd be penalized for riding with less than their capacity. You could ride a two-seater by yourself, though if you had two or fewer people on a four-seater, you'd be slapped with an additional tax. But Tatsuya and Miyuki naturally never used separate cars, so they boarded the commute train next to each other again today.

Tatsuya had opened his terminal screen and was browsing the news when a hesitant voice began:

"Tatsuya, actually, I…"

He quickly brought his head up—it wasn't like his little sister to be so inarticulate. She must have had bad news for him.

"I got a call from those people last night…" she said.

"Those people? Oh… Did Dad and the others get angry at you for some reason again?"

"No, not in particular… They seemed to at least have the good sense to choose the topic of congratulating their daughter on her enrollment. So…like I thought, Tatsuya, you didn't…?"

"Oh, that's what you meant... Nothing different here."

At those words, her face clouded, and she looked down. The next moment, he heard an angry grinding of teeth drift out of the long hair concealing her expression. "I see... I had a faint hope, despite the circumstances, but you didn't even get a single text in the end... Those people, they're just so—"

"Just calm down," soothed Tatsuya, grabbing her hand—she was trembling with such emotion that she couldn't speak.

The room temperature inside the car suddenly dropped below the regulated level—the heater activated, despite the season, and filled the silent cabin with the sound of hot air blowing.

"...I apologize. I got out of sorts."

After making sure her magic power was no longer running amok, Tatsuya let go of her hand. He lightly tapped on it a couple of times, then exchanged glances with her and smiled, as though telling her it was nothing to get hung up on.

"I ignored Dad's order to help him at the company and decided to continue school instead. Of course they can't congratulate me. You know Dad as well as I do."

"My own parents being so childish and shameless just makes my blood boil. Anyway, if they wanted to separate you from me, common sense dictates that they first inform me of that, and then our aunt. But they weren't even brave enough to do that. And apart from that, how much must those people *use* you until they're satisfied? Does it not go without saying that fifteen-year-old children go to high school?"

The bit about needing to inform their aunt and such left him with a strong sense of unease—Tatsuya had no intention of leaving Miyuki alone just because someone ordered him to—but he didn't let that show. Instead, he produced a cynical smile, purposely exaggerated and theatrical.

"It's not commonly compulsory education, so it *doesn't* go without saying. Dad and Sayuri both try to use me because they acknowledge

I'm an adult, right? If they're counting on me like that, I can't get mad at them."

"...If you say so, Tatsuya..." Miyuki nodded, though her reluctance caused Tatsuya to heave a sigh.

She didn't know exactly what the Four Leaves Technology lab, the magical-engineering-device manufacturer their father was the head of R&D at, was making him do. She was under the false assumption that they were letting him do honest work as a side job.

If she had found out he was really just being treated as a recovery tool for research materials, she might have actually frozen up the transportation system. But the commute train, ignorant of his misgivings, smoothly switched over to a lower-speed lane.

◇ ◇ ◇

The 1-E classroom was a disorderly mess as students began to arrive. The other classrooms were probably in a similar state of affairs.

It looked like there were a lot of students who had met each other yesterday, and they had already formed small groups that were making light conversation here and there.

He didn't have anyone he needed to go out of his way to greet, so he decided to look for his terminal first. As he scanned the numbers on the desks, he unexpectedly heard his name called and looked up.

"Morning!" The voice was that of Erika, bright and brimming with energy as usual.

"Good morning." Next to her, Mizuki was smiling at him, reserved but quite pleasant.

They seemed to have become fast friends. Erika was leaning on Mizuki's desk and waving her hand. They'd probably been having a conversation before they spotted him.

Tatsuya raised a hand and returned their greeting, then made his way over to them.

Shiba and Shibata—it was more alphabetical order than coincidence, but Tatsuya's seat was next to Mizuki's.

"Looks like we're next to each other again."

"Yes, that it does. I look forward to it," Mizuki replied with a smile. Then, next to her (actually, "above her" would have been accurate as well), Erika made a dissatisfied face. —Probably on purpose.

"I kinda feel left out!" Her voice had a sort of teasing echo to it.

Of course, Tatsuya wasn't cute enough to be ruffled by something like that. "It seems like it would be really hard to leave you out of anything, Chiba."

Erika squinted unhappily at his dry voice and tone. This time it didn't entirely look like an act. "...What's that supposed to mean?"

"I mean you're an extremely social person," said Tatsuya, maintaining his prim facial expression even on the receiving end of Erika's glare.

Instead, it was Erika who made a subtly regretful face. "...Shiba, you've actually got a bad character, don't you?"

After seeing Mizuki unable to suppress a smile out of the corner of his eye, Tatsuya placed his ID card on the terminal and began to review the information on it.

There was everything from elective rules, disciplinary rules, and usage rules for equipment to events that went along with enrollment, a guide to free-period activities, and the curriculum for the first semester. He scrolled through it quickly, hammering it into his head. Using only keyboard controls, he swiftly registered for courses. He had just brought his head back up to take a breath when his eyes met with a male student in the seat in front of him, whose eyes were wide and staring at his hands.

"...I don't mind you looking, but..."

"Huh? Oh, sorry. It was just unusual. Couldn't take my eyes off it."

"Is it unusual?"

"I think it is. These days, nobody uses keyboard input only. It's the first time I've seen someone do it."

"If you get used to it, this way is faster, though. Eye cursors and brain wave assistance are a little lacking in the accuracy department."

"That's just it. You're so fast. Couldn't you earn a living doing that?"

"No... I would probably only be able to get a part-time job with it."

"That so...? Whoops, forgot to introduce myself. I'm Leonhard Saijou. My dad's a half and my mom's a quarter, so I look like a pure Japanese person on the outside, but my name is Western. My specialty is convergence-type hardening magic. I hope to get a job that involves physical activity in the future, like a SWAT officer or a wilderness security officer. You can just call me Leo."

It might seem odd given the state of today's youth that someone would have already decided on a course for his future before even enrolling in high school, but magic high schools were different. The abilities—no, the very nature—of magicians (in the making) were deeply tied to their path through life. So when Leo included his future aspirations in his self-introduction, Tatsuya didn't find it surprising.

"I'm Tatsuya Shiba. You can call me Tatsuya."

"Okay, Tatsuya. What kind of magic is your forte?"

"I don't have much in the way of practical skill, so I'm aiming to become a magic engineer."

"Oh, yeah... You do look pretty smart."

Magic engineers, short for magic engineering technicians, referred to the technical experts who manufactured, developed, and adjusted devices to supplement, amplify, and strengthen magic. Without tuning from an engineer, CADs, now an essential tool for magicians, were worse than a dust-covered magical tome.

Magic engineers were a step below magicians in terms of social standing, but the business world needed them more than normal magicians. The paychecks of first-rate magic engineers even exceeded those of first-rate magicians. That being the case, it wasn't unusual that students of magic who lacked practical skill would endeavor to become magic engineers, but...

"Hm? What was that? Shiba, you want to be a magic engineer?"

"Tatsuya, who's *this*?" asked Leo, pointing a finger somewhat tentatively at Erika, who had stuck her neck in energetically as if she'd gotten wind of a big scoop.

"Wow, did you just call me *this*? And point your finger at me? You're so rude, so rude! You're a rude person! This is why guys like you aren't popular with girls."

"Wha—? You're the one being rude here! Your face might be a little *easy on the eyes*, but that doesn't mean you can run your mouth like that!"

"Looks are important, you know! But I guess a guy who can't tell the difference between looking sloppy and looking wild wouldn't understand. And what's with that expression? They only stopped using it, like, a century ago. Nobody says it anymore!"

"Wha, wha, wha...?"

Erika looked down at an angle with a composed sneer, while Leo was too dumbfounded to do much more than groan.

"...Erika, please stop. You said a little too much."

"Leo, you give it a rest, too. The same goes for you, and I don't think you can outtalk her anyway."

Tatsuya and Mizuki each interposed themselves into the volatile air.

"...If you say so, Mizuki."

"...All right, fine."

They both turned their faces away, but kept their eyes on each other.

Both strong-willed, determined, and unyielding—maybe these two are actually a good fit for each other, thought Tatsuya.

◇ ◇ ◇

The bell rang to signal the start of class, and the students, spread about wherever they pleased, returned to their seats.

This part of the system had been the same for a century, but beyond that, there were differences.

Each terminal that was still off automatically turned on, and the ones that were already booted up refreshed their windows. A message appeared on the screen in the front of the classroom at the same time.

…Orientation will begin in five minutes, so please wait in your seats. If you haven't set your ID cards in your terminals yet, please do so immediately……

The message was completely meaningless for Tatsuya. He was already at the point where he'd finished registering for his electives, and the online guidance was just a bore with too many visual effects bogging it down. Just as he decided he'd skip the whole thing and search through the school data, something unexpected occurred.

The main bell rang, and the front door opened. It wasn't a student running late—it was a young woman, not in a school uniform, but a suit.

She was pretty in her own way—though not on the level that everyone would say so without hesitation—and she had a sort of charm about her. She went before the lectern, which had risen out of the floor, placed the large portable terminal she'd been carrying at her side atop it, and looked around the classroom.

Tatsuya wasn't the only one stricken with surprise—the entire classroom was abuzz with confusion.

At schools with online classes that used a lectern terminal, teachers didn't stand at the podium and teach. Classes were conducted across the terminal. Delivering messages to classrooms was even lower on the priority list, so schools never dispatched staff members to them. The staff controls in the classroom were used only when something out of the ordinary happened—at least, in theory.

Still, it went without saying that this woman was clearly part of the faculty.

"I see there's nobody absent. Well then, everyone, congratulations on your enrollment."

There were a few students who were lured in and responded with a bow—in fact, the male student he'd just met in the seat in front of him lowered his head and said, "Thanks."

But Tatsuya couldn't help but be confused at the woman's odd behavior.

First of all, she didn't need to physically look around to check attendance. The seating situation was being monitored in real time via the ID cards set up on their terminals. School officials also didn't need to carry around terminals that large. There were consoles set up all over the school. Actually, even the lectern that had risen up from the floor should have been loaded with a console and a monitor.

And anyway, who was she? He hadn't seen anything in the enrollment information about this school utilizing the anachronistic homeroom teacher system...

"Pleased to meet you. I'm Haruka Ono, one of the general counselors working at this school. We'll be here if you need to talk about anything, and if you need a counselor more suited to a certain field, it is our job as general counselors to introduce you to them."

...Come to think of it, there was something like that...

Tatsuya had skimmed over that bit, since for him the entire idea of having someone to talk your problems out with was nonexistent. This school having a complete counseling system was one of its selling points, though.

"There are a total of sixteen general counselors in the offices. A man and woman form a pair, and one pair is assigned to each class. Mr. Yanagisawa and I are assigned to this one."

She stopped there and manipulated the console on the lectern. The upper portion of a man who looked to be in his midthirties appeared on the screen in the front of the classroom as well as on the displays on each desk.

"Pleased to meet you. I'm your other counselor, Yanagisawa. Ms. Ono and I have been assigned to this class, so I look forward to working with all of you."

Haruka—or "Ms. Ono"—began to explain again, with the counselor Yanagisawa still on the screen.

"Counseling can be conducted through the terminals like this, but we don't mind you coming in person to talk to us. All communications use quantum cryptography, and any results of counseling are stored in a stand-alone databank, so your privacy will never be invaded." As she spoke, she held up a book-shaped databank that Tatsuya had mistaken for a large portable terminal.

"We will do all we can to ensure that all of you are able to lead a fulfilling life here at school." She paused, and her superformal tone did a one eighty, becoming informal and gentle. "With that said, I'm looking forward to seeing you more!"

He could feel the energy in the classroom draining. That was some pretty fantastic emotional control—she had manipulated their levels of nervousness, even factoring her own appearance into it.

Despite her youth—she appeared to be straight out of university—she seemed very experienced. If she were to do this in a one-on-one situation, they might end up talking about things they weren't planning to. This was an important quality for a counselor, but she could probably also make it as a spy.

One worth being cautious around, thought Tatsuya.

—On the screen behind her, her older male colleague, looking more and more worried the longer he was left up there, gave a bow and the image shut off. If that hadn't happened, the impression he'd been giving would have been far stronger.

Haruka cleared her throat and reconstructed a businesslike smile, then continued to speak as if nothing had happened.

"I'm going to start the guidance for the school's curriculum and establishments on your terminals. After that, you will register for your elective courses, and orientation will be over. If there's anything you don't understand, please press the call button. Those of you who have already looked over the curriculum guide and the establishments guide can feel free to skip the guidance and go straight to registering for electives."

Haruka looked down at her lectern monitor then, and made a *hm?* face.

"...Those who have already registered for their electives can feel free to leave the room if they wish. However, once guidance has begun, you will be unable to leave the classroom, so if anyone wants to do so, please leave the room now. And don't forget your ID cards when you go."

A chair clattered, as if waiting for those words.

It wasn't Tatsuya.

The one who stood up was a slender, high-strung young man. He sat a bit away from Tatsuya, in the front row at the window. He bowed toward the lectern, then turned his back to the classroom and exited to the hallway.

He left the classroom haughtily, appearing to act tough, not paying attention to the upturned gazes gathering on him from both sides. It drew Tatsuya's interest, but only for a moment. Aside from Tatsuya, about half the class watched his back as he left, but their stares soon returned to the lectern.

It didn't look like any others would leave early. It wasn't as if Tatsuya disliked the place so much that he'd do something so conspicuous to get out of it.

He looked back at his hands, stopped on the keyboard, and wondered what to browse to pass the time, when suddenly he felt eyes on him and looked back up.

Haruka was looking at him from the lectern.

Even when their eyes met, she made no attempt to avert hers, and smiled sweetly at him.

* * *

What was that all about…?

He noticed it after that, too—Haruka was smiling at him. Not the whole time, though—she did it with short, reserved glances so the other students wouldn't harbor suspicion, but it still created an air of excessive secrecy.

He could say for sure this was the first time they'd met.

It was clearly too frequent to be a merely friendly smile, so Tatsuya tried stepping back through his memories to figure it out. That used up a lot of time, but…

That wasn't…her trying to get me to relax, was it? It seemed more like something to unsettle me… And I don't think that a member of the faculty would be hitting on a student in the classroom, even if she isn't a teacher…

As far as he could think, it was probably her being interested in Tatsuya for remaining in his seat even though he had finished registering just like the student who left had. But he still felt like it was still a fairly *confidential* smile, to put it in a positive light.

As he was puzzling over it, a voice addressed him from the seat in front of him.

"Tatsuya, what are you gonna do until lunch?"

Leo was looking at him, straddling his chair with his hands over its back and resting his chin on it, almost as if it were his regular pose. It was the exact same way he'd done it last time.

Eating lunch in the classroom was no longer a tradition in junior high schools and high schools. Information terminals were sensitive devices despite advances in waterproofing and dust-proofing tech. If you accidentally spilled soup on one, things could end up a disastrous mess.

Should he go to the cafeteria, to the courtyard, to the roof, to a clubroom—or should he just find any old place? It was more than an hour until the cafeteria opened.

"I had planned to stare at the catalog of information right here… but okay, I'll come with you."

Leo's eyes, sparkling with fun, clouded with disappointment at what Tatsuya said. He smiled wryly at Leo's truly transparent expressions and nodded. "Where should we go see, then?"

Magic wasn't taught in public schools until after junior high school. Children with an aptitude for magic learned the basics at public cram school after regular school hours. At that stage, the children weren't judged based on how good or bad their magical technique was—it was purely to further their potential. Whether or not they had the talent to walk the path of magic as a living was something decided by the students themselves and their parents or guardians. There were certain private schools that included magical education as an extracurricular activity, but magic went assiduously unnoted on students' grades.

Serious magic education started at the high school level, and though First High was counted among the most difficult magic high schools to get into, this meant that there were many students who had advanced here from a normal junior high school. The upper-level, magic-related courses would have contained classes that those students had never seen before.

Today and tomorrow, the school had built time into the day to let students observe the classrooms they'd be in. It was to relieve some of the worries of the new students unfamiliar with such courses.

"Wanna go to the workshop?"

Tatsuya's question to Leo's response was this: "Not the arena?"

Leo grinned in a satisfied way at the unexpected inquiry. "I guess I do come off that way, huh? Well, you're not wrong, but…"

On average, the students here would be intelligent. They had gotten into this school in the first place, after all. But this young man was—how should he put it? He was brimming with energy—he seemed like the outdoor type, or something. Frankly speaking, he came off like a rascal. It made him feel like he was more suited for going all-out in the arena than fiddling with sensitive devices in the workshop, and Tatsuya probably wasn't the only one.

But upon hearing the next thing Leo said, he acknowledged his false impression.

"Hardening magic is most efficient when you pair it with weapon techniques, after all. I want to at least be able to take care of my own weapons by myself."

"I see..."

Leo's career of choice was a policeman—and a SWAT officer or member of a wilderness security force, at that. It things went as he hoped, he would have plenty of opportunities to use simple shields and weapons like batons, axes, and hatchets. Those tools had good affinity with hardening magic, and its effectiveness varied greatly depending on whether you were familiar with the properties of the materials making up the weapons.

His classmate seemed to have a far more grounded and realistic idea of his own aptitude and course for the future than he let on.

As the two of them finished their conversation, a shy request to join them came from the seat next to him. "If you're going to see the workshop, may I go with you?"

"Shibata, you wanna go there too?" Erika interrupted from past Mizuki's head.

"Yes... I want to be a magic engineer as well."

"Ah, that makes some kinda sense!"

In the same way he had before, Leo gave an affected grimace. "You're more the type to do physical labor, aren't you? Just go to the arena or something."

"I don't want to hear that from you, you wild animal."

Tit for tat.

"What was that? You were thinking of that one all day long, weren't you?"

They always seemed to get into arguments right away. "Stop it, you two... You just met today."

I still think they're actually rather compatible, thought Tatsuya, breathing a sigh and trying to mediate, but it didn't stop that easily.

"Heh, I bet we were bitter enemies in a past life."

"Yeah, you were a bear wrecking the farmlands or something, and I was the hunter they hired to exterminate you."

Mizuki had been meekly keeping out of it, but she had finally given up on this ending anytime soon, so she attempted a forced change of course. "Let's get going! We'll run out of time!"

Tatsuya took advantage of the opportunity without a moment's delay. "You're right! If we don't go soon, we'll be the last ones left in the classroom."

Interrupted by their fast talking, Leo and Erika glared at each other in displeasure, then immediately both turned away.

◇ ◇ ◇

Even on the second day, people were already solidifying into groups to move around in together. Maybe this was a quick adjustment, or maybe it was hasty, and perhaps it was only natural—Tatsuya didn't know. But when he thought about whether he'd drawn a good lot, he decided that he had, in all probability.

Erika and Leo were both bright and outgoing, and Mizuki, while shy, seemed to have an easygoing personality. He was aware of his tendency to sink into cynicism, so he considered himself lucky that they had been the first friends he'd made at high school.

But "in all probability" didn't mean 100 percent.

Those few percentage points that remained...

I'm very glad and everything that they aren't obsequious, but can't they do something about this? wondered Tatsuya calmly.

"Tatsuya..."

On the other hand, Miyuki was grabbing Tatsuya's uniform cuff with her fingers, looking up at his face with a mixture of perplexity and unease.

"Don't apologize for anything, Miyuki. This isn't even 0.1 percent

your fault," replied Tatsuya, purposely in a strong voice, to encourage
his sister.

"Yes, but... Will you stop them?"

"...That would probably have the opposite effect."

"...Yes, perhaps. But still, I was rather surprised... Erika seemed
the type, but to think Mizuki had that kind of personality as well..."

"...Same here."

Watching over them from a few steps away—or maybe just watching them—the siblings' eyes reflected a group of new students, split
into two, glaring at each other in a volatile atmosphere. One group
was Miyuki's classmates, and the members making up the other were,
of course, Mizuki, Erika, and Leo.

Act 1 had occurred in the cafeteria at lunchtime.

The First High cafeteria was rather large for a high school, but it
would always get crowded at this time of year, because the new students didn't know what was going on yet.

But Tatsuya and the others, who had left their observation of an
upper-level course early and come to the cafeteria, secured a four-seat
table without much trouble.

It seated four, but it was just two benches facing each other; you
could probably fit three slender female students on one side.

When they were about halfway done with their food (Leo had
already finished), Miyuki arrived in the cafeteria surrounded by both
male and female classmates, saw Tatsuya, and hurried over to him.

That was the first bit of trouble—that Miyuki tried to eat with
him. She wasn't an eccentric who refused to mingle with her classmates, but in her mind, Tatsuya was the top priority.

Only one other person could sit at this table. Miyuki didn't give
her choice between her classmates or Tatsuya a second thought.

But of course, her classmates, especially the male ones, wanted to
share a table with her.

At first, they used indirect expressions like "There's no room" or "I don't want to bother them." Upon seeing how unexpectedly strongly fixated Miyuki was on this, some ended up saying things like "We shouldn't share a table with Course 2 students" or "We should make a distinction between Course 1 and Course 2 students." One even demanded Leo vacate his seat, since he'd finished eating.

Leo and Erika were on the verge of lashing out at the Course 1 students' selfish, arrogant remarks. Tatsuya quickly finished eating, said something to Leo, informed Erika and Mizuki—who were still eating—and got up from his seat.

Miyuki apologized with her eyes to Tatsuya and the other three and, without sitting at the table that now had one empty side, walked away in the opposite direction.

Act 2 had been an event during an observation of an upper-level course that afternoon.

Class 3-A was having a test of practical skill in the long-range magic practice room, affectionately dubbed the "shooting range." It was the class the student president Mayumi Saegusa was a member of.

Students weren't necessarily picked for the student council based on grades, but she was considered the kind of genius at long-range precise magic that came around only every ten years, and she had brought enough trophies to First High to back that up.

New students had heard the rumors about her as well. And they had seen her look more coquettish than those rumors at the entrance ceremony.

A large number of new students packed into the firing range to witness her skills, but only so many of them were able to observe it. When it came to it, amidst many Course 2 students giving their spots to Course 1 students, Tatsuya and the others boldly positioned themselves in the front row.

So of course, they were seen as obtrusive.

* * *

And Act 3 was now occurring, with Mizuki speaking in sharp tones just as they were leaving.

"Would you please just give up? Miyuki said she's going home with her brother. Strangers shouldn't be arguing with her about that."

She was speaking to a student from 1-A. It was one of the faces they'd seen in the cafeteria during lunch break.

Basically, two of Miyuki's classmates had been clinging to her as she waited for Tatsuya after school, and one had taken issue with him. Incidentally, that classmate was a girl. Meanwhile, the male student, as one would expect, had remained silent at the beginning, probably because he was worried about stares from others (or maybe Miyuki's). But now, their restraint—or perhaps his common sense—had left the area.

"Miyuki isn't treating you like nuisances, is she? If you wanted to go home with her, then you should just come along. What right do you have to tear the two of them apart?"

Unexpectedly, Mizuki was the first one to snap at the Course 1 students' irrational actions. She kept her demeanor polite, but her logic was merciless as she delivered her oratory without taking even one step back from the Blooms she was speaking to.

Yes, at first it was logical, but…

"Tear us apart…?" murmured Tatsuya from a little ways away. He got the feeling that something was decisively *off* about that.

"M-Mizuki must be misunderstanding something, right?" After hearing her brother murmur, Miyuki started to get flustered for some reason.

"Miyuki… Why are you the one panicking?"

"Huh? No, I'm not flustered at all, am I?"

"And why do you keep asking questions?"

Glancing at the siblings who were central to this trouble as they were moving into a rather confusing situation, their "extremely considerate" friends were getting more and more heated up.

"We have something to talk to her about!" That was male classmate number one of Miyuki's.

"That's right! I'm sorry, Mr. Shiba, but we just need to borrow her for a bit!" That was female classmate number one of Miyuki's.

Leo burst out laughing at their selfish complaints. "Hah! Do that during your free period. They put time aside for stuff like that, you know."

Erika put on her best sarcastic face and tone and followed up. "Why don't you get the person's consent beforehand if you had something to talk to them about? You can't just ignore Miyuki's wishes and have a big discussion with her. Those are the rules. You're in high school now—you know that, right?"

Erika's words and attitude were meant to make them angry. It did just that—male student number one snapped. "Shut up! People from other classes, and Weeds at that, shouldn't be messing with us Blooms!"

School rules forbade the usage of the term *Weed* on the grounds that it was discriminatory. It was a rule in name more than reality, but it still wasn't a term to be used in a situation where this many people were listening.

The one who responded to that outburst head-on was—and this was not necessarily a surprise—Mizuki.

"Aren't we all new students? How much better do you Blooms think you are at this point in time, anyway?" She wasn't raising her voice by any stretch, but it still strangely reverberated through the schoolyard.

"...Uh-oh. This isn't good," Tatsuya thought aloud as a mumble. It was drowned out by the Course 1 student's stifled voice, and only Miyuki, who was next to him, heard it.

"...If you want to know, then I'll show you how much better we are!"

Mizuki's claim was correct, based on the rules of the school, but at the same time, it was in a way rejecting the school's system.

"Hah, that's funny! Come on, give us a lesson!" Leo called out provocatively upon hearing the Course 1 student's words, which could be taken either as a threat or an ultimatum. The situation had already reached a point where nothing could be done, so it didn't do any good to mention it now, but he and Erika were in complete "tit for tat" mode.

Mizuki had the truth on her side. They knew it, too. That's why those who lived comfortably within the current system—students and teachers alike—would respond emotionally.

Even if there was a clear breach of the rules here, unless it came from Mizuki's side, most people would probably pretend they didn't see it.

Even if it wasn't only a breach of school rules—but against the law.

"Then I'll show you!"

The only students permitted to carry their CADs inside school were the student council members and members of certain clubs.

Usage of magic outside school was strictly controlled by the law. However, possessing a CAD outside of school wasn't forbidden. There would be no point.

CADs were currently an essential item for magicians, but they were not absolutely necessary to perform magic. One could use magic without a CAD. So just owning one wasn't against the law.

Because of this, the school made students possessing CADs leave them in the office when classes began and come back to get them when they left school. Also because of this, students having CADs when going home from school wasn't really that strange.

"A specialized type?"

But pointing one at another student was not a normal situation. In fact, it was an emergency—especially if the CAD being pointed was a specialized type focusing on attack power.

Casting Assistant Devices were split into two categories: multipurpose and specialized. Multipurpose ones could store a maximum of ninety-nine types of activation programs, but it put a large burden on the user. Specialized ones could hold only nine types, but they were fitted with subsystems to lighten the load on the user, allowing him or her to cast magic more quickly.

On top of that characteristic, there were many specialized CADs that stored activation programs for offensive magic.

With the shrieks of onlookers as background music, he stuck the "barrel" of his pistol-shaped, specialized CAD in Leo's face.

This student wasn't all bark. His skill at drawing his CAD, the speed at which he aimed—both were clearly the movements of a magic technician experienced in the ways of battle.

Much of magic depended on innate talent. That meant that at the same time, a lot in magic depended on your lineage. If you were a Course 1 student who had enrolled in this school with excellent grades, then even if you hadn't received any magical education in school, you were more than likely to have received real combat experience from helping parents, family businesses, and relatives.

"Tatsuya!"

Before Miyuki had finished calling out, Tatsuya had already stuck out his right hand. He reached out, though his hand wouldn't reach her from this distance.

Did the action mean something? Or was it a pointless reflex, created outside the realm of conscious thought? Whatever it was, here and now, it didn't have any effect, because...

"Eeegh!"

The one who shrieked was the Course 1 student jabbing the gun in Leo's face.

His pistol-shaped CAD had been sent flying out of his hand.

And before his eyes was Erika, smiling, having whipped out an extending police baton from somewhere. There was no lingering waver or panic in her grin. But he'd known from the start there had been none of that, just by seeing her skillful alertness, which almost gave away her personality. If the same thing happened a hundred more times, Erika would without a doubt smack the CAD out of the

Course 1 student's hand with her baton every single time. He could clearly see that ability in her.

"At this distance, whoever moves their body first is fastest."

"Yes, but you were totally trying to hit my hand, too, weren't you?"

No sooner had Erika let down her guard than she had returned to her nonserious demeanor and began to explain it proudly to him. Answering her was Leo, who had pulled his hand—which was about to grab the CAD—away at the last moment.

"Oh, no! I wouldn't do anything like that." Erika flashed a smile that *might* have been evasive, as though she might have instead put the back of her hand holding the baton to her mouth and gone *Oh-ho-ho-ho!*

Leo's patience with her was wearing extremely thin. "You're not fooling anyone with that dumb grin!"

"I'm serious. I can tell whether or not someone can dodge based on how they carry themselves. You may look like an idiot, but you seem like you have skill."

"...You're making fun of me, aren't you? You're making a complete fool out of me, aren't you?"

"Well, I did just say you looked like an idiot, didn't I?"

Forgetting about the "enemy" in front of them, the two of them went back and forth loudly, like a comedy routine. Tatsuya, Miyuki, and everybody else around were too amazed to say much. Miyuki's classmate was the one who snapped out of it first and faced them.

It wasn't the male student who had the specialized device knocked out of his hands—it was the female student behind him, whose fingers flew over her multipurpose bracelet CAD.

The systems inside sprang to life, and an activation program began to expand.

Activation programs were the blueprints for magic. The programming within directly defined how to formulate magic programs. Once it was finished expanding the activation program, it would then read it into the user's magic calculation region, an unconscious location in their brain. It would input the values for the variables that denoted coordinates, output, and duration. Finally, it would build up the psions—and the magic program—according to the process described in the activation program.

The calculation region of the person's subconscious would construct the magic program and then transfer it through a route between the lowest level of consciousness and the highest level of unconsciousness. Then the magic program would be projected from the gate existing between consciousness and unconsciousness into the external world of information. Thus would the magic program interfere with the projection's target, the information bodies incident to events—in modern magic, these were referred to as eidos, from a Greek philosophy term—and temporarily overwrite the target's information.

Information accompanied events. If you overwrote the information, you would overwrite the event. The state of events described in the psionic information bodies would temporarily alter the event in the real world.

This was the magical system that made use of CADs.

The speed at which psion information bodies were constructed was the user's *magical throughput*. The scale at which the information bodies could be formulated was the user's *magical capacity*. The intensity at which the magical program overwrote the eidos was the user's *influence*. Currently, the three of these together were referred to as one's magical power.

The activation programs that were the blueprints of magic were a type of psionic information body as well. However, they themselves couldn't effect change in events. The CADs would convert the psions injected from the user into signals, then return an activation program to the user.

Broadly speaking, this was the function of a CAD. With the psionic information body (the activation program) supplied from the CAD as a base, the magician would construct a psionic information body (the magic program) to overwrite events.

Many specialized types were shaped like guns. The advantage to this was that they had an alignment support system on the part corresponding to the gun barrel. This system would embed coordinate information into the activation program when it was expanded. In doing so, it would lighten the computation load for the user.

From the magician to the CAD, and from the CAD to the magician.

If this psionic flow was obstructed, any magic using the CAD would cease to function.

For example, if you hit it with a clump of psions from the outside while the activation program was being deployed or being read, the psionic pattern constructing the activation program would be corrupted, it would fail to build a functional magic program, and the magic would fizzle.

And that was exactly what happened.

"Stop this at once! Attacking another person with magic outside of self-defensive purposes is not only against school rules but a criminal act!"

The activation program being expanded by the female student's CAD had been blown apart by a psionic bullet.

Forming psions themselves into bullets and firing them was the simplest form of magic, but the delicate precision and controlled output of destroying only the activation program and not causing any damage to the caster herself spoke volumes of the shooter's skill.

Recognizing the voice's owner, the female student trying to attack Erika and the others went pale with shock—and it wasn't because of the magic. She staggered as another female student held her up from behind.

The one who had delivered the warning and used a psionic bullet to stop the magic from executing had been the student council president, Mayumi Saegusa.

Her expression, which was normally a smile—as far as Tatsuya knew—was still not very strict, even in this situation.

But the eyes of those who used magic saw the light of energized psions, and it was obviously far larger in scale than the light given off by average magicians. It wrapped around her small body like a nimbus, giving her a sort of impenetrable majesty.

"You're all from 1-A and 1-E, right? I'll listen to what you have to say. Come with me."

The one who gave the order in a cold—well, it had to be—and hard voice was the female student standing next to Mayumi. According to the student introductions during the entrance ceremony, she was the head of the disciplinary committee, a senior named Mari Watanabe.

Mari's CAD has already finished expanding an activation program. It was easy to imagine that if they showed any signs of resistance, she would use force instantly.

Leo, Mizuki, and Miyuki's classmates all stiffened without a word. It wasn't that they couldn't move out of rebelliousness, but that they had been overawed by her. Leaving his classmates aside...

...without puffing out his chest with pride or arrogance...

...without hanging his head in dejection or atrophy...

...Tatsuya walked before Mari with a composed gait, with Miyuki gracefully following behind him.

Mari gave a quizzical look at the freshmen who had suddenly appeared. Tatsuya and Miyuki hadn't appeared to her to be part of all this. Tatsuya, unperturbed, returned her gaze and gave a slight but polite bow.

"I'm sorry. We let our horseplay go too far."

"Horseplay?" Mari's eyebrows pulled into a frown at the statement, which seemed abrupt.

"Yes. The Morisaki family is famous for its quick-drawing, so I wanted him to show us for future reference, but it was so lifelike and real that we accidentally reacted."

The male student who had aimed his CAD at Leo—his eyes were widened in astonishment.

As the other freshmen looked on, speechless now for a different reason, Mari glanced between the baton in Erika's hand and the gun-shaped device that had fallen to the ground. She turned her gaze on the boy and girl who had attempted to use their CADs in an illegal way, and after seeing them start to tremble, she shot a cold smile at Tatsuya.

"Then after that, why did the girl from 1-A execute an attack magic?"

"She was probably surprised. She's able to execute the activation process out of pure conditioned reflex—that's a Course 1 student for you." His expression was totally serious, but his voice was completely transparent.

"Your friends were about to be attacked by magic. Are you still going to claim this was just horseplay?"

"You say *attack*, but all she was actually planning to activate was a bright magic flash to distract us. And it wasn't high-enough level to cause blindness or impair our eyesight permanently, anyway."

Everyone gasped again.

Her scornful smile turned into an expression of astonishment. "Impressive... You seem to be able to read and understand expanded activation programs."

Activation programs were vast clumps of data for constructing magic programs.

Magicians could intuitively understand what sort of effects a magic program possessed.

During the process where a magic program interferes with eidos, a magician could "read" what sort of alteration the magic program was trying to achieve by the reaction given from the eidos, which resisted the alteration.

But the activation program was nothing more than a cluster of data on its own. And it was an immense amount of data, too. Even the magician who expanded it would only be able to semiautomatically process it unconsciously.

Reading an activation program was like being able to visualize an image in your head by looking only at the digits making up the image's data. Normally you couldn't understand such a thing consciously.

"My practical abilities are subpar, but analysis is a specialty of mine."

But Tatsuya summed up the abnormal ability as simply *analysis*, as if it didn't mean anything.

"...And deception is apparently another."

Mari's stare was somewhere between an appraisal and a glare.

Only Miyuki stepped in front of her brother, as if to shield him from taking the brunt of it. "As my brother said, this was really just a minor misunderstanding. We deeply apologize for getting our upper-classmen involved."

Without a scrap of artifice, she bowed deeply directly to Mari who, taken aback, averted her eyes.

"Mari, isn't that enough? Tatsuya, this was really just a practical observation, right?"

Since when are we on a first-name basis? thought Tatsuya, but he couldn't let the lifeboat Mayumi offered him go unused.

As before, he nodded his head in all earnestness, and Mayumi gave a somehow proud smile—almost as if to say *You owe me one.*

"It certainly isn't against the rules for students to teach one another, but there are detailed restrictions on even executing magic. This is something taught in class during the first semester. I believe it would be best for now to refrain from any self-study that involves activating magic."

Her serious expression returned as she conferred her directive. Then Mari, as well, delivered her judgment, using carefully chosen words.

"...The president has spoken, so I won't question you this time. Make sure this doesn't happen again." Without sparing a glance at the group of students, who were bitter enemies but all hastily straightening up and bowing to her together, Mari turned on her heel.

But she had taken only one step before she stopped and asked a question, her back still to them.

"What is your name?"

Only her head was facing him, and her eyes were thin slits, their edges reflecting Tatsuya in them.

"Tatsuya Shiba, from Class 1-E."

"I'll remember it."

He was about to say *Fine by me* out of reflex, but he caught himself and stopped himself from sighing.

◇ ◇ ◇

"...I don't consider this a *debt*, you know."

After watching the officials disappear into the school building, the first person who made a violent move—in other words, the male student from Class 1-A, whom Tatsuya had ended up covering for— shot him a thorny stare, and with an equally thorny tone of voice, said that to Tatsuya.

Tatsuya sighed and looked behind him. All of his friends were making the same face, too. Relieved that their uselessly excitable personalities weren't here, at least, he returned the thorny 1-A student's gaze.

"Don't worry. I don't believe I gave you anything anyway. It wasn't my words that decided this, but Miyuki's good faith."

"Tatsuya may be good at talking people down, but he's not so good at persuading people," remarked Miyuki.

"You're not wrong." He returned her feigned stare of criticism with a dry smile.

"...My name is Shun Morisaki. As you deduced, I'm part of the main Morisaki family."

The hostility in his face thinned a bit, his spirit perhaps dampened at the siblings' heartwarming—depending on how you looked at it—exchange.

"Well, it wasn't anything so grandiose as a *deduction*. I've just seen an example video of it before."

"Oh, come to think of it, I might have seen that, too," remarked Erika.

"And you just didn't remember it until now? You really are different from Tatsuya," said Leo.

"Don't sound so self-important. You're such an idiot that you tried to grab a *broom* with your bare hands! Your head is what's different!"

"What was that? Why do you keep calling me an idiot?"

"Umm... It really was dangerous. Activation programs made by the psions of other magicians could cause rejection in your magic calculation region..." mentioned Miyuki.

"There, see? Understand now?" agreed Erika.

"But you too, Erika. Even if you didn't directly touch it with your hands, it could still interfere with you."

"I'm fine! This thing's shielded."

His friends' conversation behind him had begun to take on meaning, but Tatsuya remained where he was, eyes locked with Morisaki.

"I won't accept you, Tatsuya Shiba. Your sister should be with us."

With a parting threat, he turned his back without waiting for a reply. Parting threats didn't need responses in the first place—since they were parting threats—but they did require the other person to hear them.

"Using my full name like that already, I see," he said, almost as though he were talking to himself, but purposely murmuring loud enough for him to hear. Morisaki, turned away, gave a start. A certain kind of stubbornness was probably what allowed him to keep going and leave without stopping.

Next to him, Miyuki looked bewildered when she heard Tatsuya allow his muttering to be overheard. She was always fretting over this—for someone with such an introspective personality, he had a self-destructive recklessness. He wouldn't hesitate to make enemies, and it was a big flaw in his character. Of course, she was more disconcerted about Morisaki's mistaken impression.

"Tatsuya, shouldn't we go home soon?"

"You're right. Leo, Chiba, Shibata, let's get going."

In any case, the two of them shared their feeling of mental exhaustion, nodded to each other, and decided to leave.

The girl from 1-A who was about to make the situation worse was standing in their way, but he honestly didn't want to get any more involved with her today. He exchanged looks with Miyuki and went to pass her by. Miyuki, trying to guess Tatsuya's feelings, was about to say *See you tomorrow* when the girl opened her mouth first.

"I'm Honoka Mitsui. I apologize for being rude earlier."

She suddenly bowed to Tatsuya, and frankly, he was taken aback. Until now, her attitude hadn't been able to fully conceal her sense of being an elite—and that was an understatement—but now it had flip-flopped.

"Thank you for covering for me. Morisaki may have said that, but it's because of you, sir, that it didn't escalate."

"...You're welcome. But don't call me 'sir.' We're still both freshmen."

"I understand. Then what should I call you...?"

Her eyes looked like she was bent on this.

I hope this doesn't come back to bite me, he thought, but being careful not to let any irritation into his voice, he answered, "Just Tatsuya is fine."

"...I understand. And, well..." she replied.

"...What is it?" he asked.

As the result of a quick eye contact, Miyuki placed herself in front of Honoka.

"...May I come with you to the station?"

Timidly, and yet with a certain determination in her face, Honoka had requested to go with them.

Erika and Mizuki exchanged glances—the look on her face was more surprising than her words. Though neither they nor Leo, nor

Tatsuya nor Miyuki, of course, had any reason to refuse her, and no grounds to do so anyway.

◇ ◇ ◇

The situation on the way back to the station was complicated.

They were the four members from 1-E—Tatsuya, Mizuki, Erika, and Leo—and those from 1-A—Miyuki, Honoka, and the female student who had caught Honoka when she nearly fell over at Mayumi's appearance, a girl named Shizuku Kitayama.

Next to Tatsuya was Miyuki, and Honoka had taken up her position on the other side of him for some reason.

"...Then Tatsuya does the tuning on your assistant, Miyuki?"

"Yes. Letting my brother do it gives me the most peace of mind," answered Miyuki proudly, as if it applied to her, in response to Honoka's question.

"I just tweak it a bit, though. Miyuki has high throughput, so it's not hard to do maintenance on her CAD."

"But still, you can't do that without knowing all about the device's OS." Mizuki poked her face out from beside Miyuki and entered the conversation. Tatsuya's rather forced smile didn't seem to have much effect.

"You also need the skill to access the CAD's basic systems. That's really something," remarked Leo.

"Tatsuya, maybe you could take a look at my broom, too?" piped in Erika.

He turned around to the two of them.

Erika had switched from calling him "Shiba" to calling him "Tatsuya," declaring unilaterally that if he let Mitsui do that, she could, too. And as a truly generous bargaining point, she said that in exchange, he could just call her Erika. Of course, Mizuki requested the same deal, so it had already become an established fact.

"No way. I'm not confident enough to mess around with such a unique CAD."

"Aha! You really are amazing, Tatsuya."

It was difficult to know whether Tatsuya's reply was serious or it was just him being modest, but Erika responded with unadulterated praise.

"What?"

"You knew that this was a broom."

Erika smiled brightly and spun the strap of the baton with the extending hilt around her finger at Tatsuya's question. But there was a glint of something other than a simple smile in her eyes.

"Huh? That baton is a device?"

As if that had been what she'd actually been wanting, Erika nodded twice when she saw Mizuki's eyes grow wide. "Thanks for the normal reaction, Mizuki. If everyone had figured it out, I don't know what I would have done!"

Leo asked, even more puzzled than before after hearing this exchange. He asked, "...Where is the system in that, anyway? From how it felt before, it's not completely hollow, right?"

"Bzzt. Everything but the handle is totally hollow. It makes seal techniques more powerful. Hardening magic is your specialty, isn't it?"

"...Converting spells into geometric patterns, carving them into a sensitive alloy, and injecting psions into it to activate it—those seals? Doesn't using stuff like that take a ton more psions than normal? It's a wonder you don't run out of gas. And besides, I thought seal magic was too energy-inefficient and wasn't used much anymore," pointed out Leo.

Erika opened her eyes a bit wider, her face displaying half surprise and half admiration. "Oh, look at you, such a specialist. But unfortunately, there's one more step. The only moments strength is needed are at the very beginning and when you fire. If you channel the psions precisely at those moments, it doesn't drain that much. It's the same principle as helm splitting... Hey, what's wrong, you guys?"

asked Erika uncomfortably, stricken with a blend of admiration both good and bad.

"Erika... Don't people refer to helm splitting as an almost super-human technique? It's far more amazing than just having a lot of psions," Miyuki answered for everyone.

Despite her casual remark, Erika's face stiffened up—she actually seemed as if she was getting flustered.

"Tatsuya and Miyuki are both amazing, but I guess Erika is amazing too... I wonder if normal people are the rarity at our school?" remarked Miyuki spontaneously.

"I don't think there *are* any normal people at Magic High School," returned Shizuku Kitayama—who had been silent up until now—absentmindedly, but she was right on the mark. With that, the meaningful basis of their conversation disappeared without a trace.

[3]

The train station used by First High was simply called First High Station. It was a nearly straight path from there to the school.

With how trains had changed, midtrip train transfer meetings didn't happen anymore. But for this school at least, walking with friends from the station to the school was a frequent occurrence.

He'd already seen many examples of that yesterday—the second day of school—and he'd even witnessed it multiple times this very morning.

Still, what is this? It's just too sudden, thought Tatsuya.

"Tatsuya… Were you acquainted with the president?" asked Mizuki.

"We just met the day before yesterday on the day of the entrance ceremony… At least, I'm pretty sure we did." Tatsuya himself cocked his head in puzzlement at Mizuki's question.

"Sure doesn't look like it," commented Leo.

"She's running all the way here!" added Erika.

Tatsuya had confidence in his memory. He could positively assert that he and Mayumi Saegusa had first met the day before yesterday.

But as his friends had said, she definitely wasn't acting like she had just met him.

"…Maybe she's coming to invite you, Miyuki?" suggested Tatsuya.

"…She called out your name, though," noted Miyuki.

Surrounding him were Mizuki, Erika, and Leo—the group he could already call "the usual" without it feeling strange.

They had done the same yesterday. Just as Tatsuya had come to school with Miyuki, as he had always done until now, the three of them called out to him one after another as if lying in wait for him—one while he was inside the station, another as soon as he left the station, and the third directly after that—and joined up with them.

As far as things went, he didn't dislike it or anything. It was a nice way to start off the day.

But as the five of them leisurely walked the rather short path to the school gates, a voice called out "Tatsuya!" If it had been anyone else, they surely would have been embarrassed by it. As soon as he identified the petite girl jogging over to him, he just knew (without proof) that today was going to be another stormy day.

"Morning, Tatsuya! And good morning to you as well, Miyuki."

Tatsuya felt that her treatment of him was rather rude compared to Miyuki, but she was a senior and the student council president.

"Good morning, President." He needed to endeavor to respond with suitable politeness. After Tatsuya, Miyuki showed her a polite bow.

The other three gave greetings that were more or less polite, but they couldn't help but be rather hesitant. Being nervous in this kind of situation was more normal.

"Are you by yourself, President?" He knew the answer just by looking, but he was also asking whether she was planning on following along with them like this.

"Yup. I don't particularly meet up with anyone in the morning." Her affirmation also confirmed the implied question.

But...she was still acting overfamiliar toward him.

"I had something I wanted to talk about with you as well, Miyuki... Would you mind if I came with you all?" Those words were directed at Miyuki.

She was still speaking rather informally now, but the way it sounded was different.

And apparently that wasn't just Tatsuya's imagination.

"No, I don't mind, but…"

"Oh, I'm not trying to tell you anything confidential. Or shall I wait until later?" she asked, smiling and looking at the other three, who were standing rigidly a few feet away. They expressed with words and gestures that she could feel free, and Mayumi bowed to them and another smile escaped her lips. Tatsuya, however, couldn't help but look glum.

"President… Is it just me, or are you treating one of us a little differently?"

"What? Oh, my, was I?"

Sure, *now* she changed how she spoke—but even if she played dumb, her tone and expression gave it away. Tatsuya wasn't one to get angry over this much, but that isn't to say he didn't feel any stress.

Miyuki hastily brought the conversation back to her. "What did you want to talk about? The student council?"

"Yes. I'd just like to explain it at ease at some point. Might you have any plans for lunch?"

"I think I'll be eating in the cafeteria."

"With Tatsuya?"

"No—he's in a different class, so…"

She probably remembered what happened yesterday. Mayumi nodded a few times to Miyuki's reserved answer with a look implying she knew how it was. "There are a lot of students bothered by the strangest things."

Tatsuya glanced beside him. As he expected, Mizuki was nodding along. It looked like she was still hung up on what happened yesterday.

But, President, wouldn't you saying that cause controversy? thought Tatsuya to himself.

"Then why don't you have lunch with me in the student council room? You can bring your lunch box, and there's a vending machine, too."

"…Is there a dining server placed in the student council room?" replied the normally serene Miyuki, without being able to conceal her surprise.

Her surprise wasn't only the positive kind, either.

Why would an automatic waiting machine, the sort usually placed in unmanned airport cafeterias and dining cars on long-distance trains, be stationed in a high school student council room?

"I'd rather not say too much before having you in there, but we do end up working late some days." Mayumi smiled awkwardly, a little embarrassed, and continued with her invitation. "And if it's the student council room, then there's no problem with Tatsuya coming with you."

At that time, just for a moment, Tatsuya *thought* he saw her smile change to a sly one—or an evil one, more frankly. Regardless of her expression, though, her remark had still been troubling.

"...Yes, there is. I'd rather not have any trouble with the vice president." He had no intention of interfering with his sister's student council activities, but Tatsuya had to get a word in.

The male student who had given him that glare from behind Mayumi on the day of the entrance ceremony must have been the second-year vice president.

There was no mistaking that sort of glare. If he were to casually go and eat lunch in the student council room, there was no doubt in his mind the young man would pick a fight with him.

"The vice president...?" Mayumi's head tilted to one side, and then she theatrically clapped her hands together. "You mean Hanzou? You don't need to worry about him."

"...Are you referring to Vice President Hattori?"

"Yes, why?"

At that moment, Tatsuya strongly resolved himself to never give Mayumi a reason to give him a nickname.

"Hanzou always eats lunch in his club room." Mayumi, of course, continued her solicitation without dropping her bright smile, and without a care for those thoughts of Tatsuya's. "If you like, everyone else may come with you as well. It's my role as a member of the student council to inform people of our activities, after all."

However, Mayumi's sociable offer was met by a refusal in the direct opposite tone of voice. "Thanks for the offer, but I think we'll pass."

It was an awfully blunt way of refusing her.

The atmosphere began to take a turn for the worse because of Erika's unexpected attitude. But as long as Tatsuya didn't know what she truly thought, he could neither overturn it nor follow up on it.

"I see."

The only one that didn't change was Mayumi, who still smiled.

It seemed less that she was dense and more that she was aware of circumstances they were not... Tatsuya had no particular reason for that guess, but it was still his guess.

"Then, what about just you and Tatsuya?"

Miyuki looked at him, her eyes asking what they should do. It would have been fine for him to refuse until just now, but considering the attitude Erika had just taken, refusing without coming off as abrasive would be difficult.

"...I understand. Miyuki and I will take you up on the offer."

"Is that so? That's good. Then we'll leave the details for then. I'll be waiting!" Mayumi spun around and nearly skipped away.

What is so much fun for her? Despite headed for the same school building, the five that saw her off plodded along.

A sigh escaped Tatsuya's lips.

◇ ◇ ◇

Lunch break came quickly.

His feet felt like lead. But his conditioning wasn't so poor that he would get exhausted just from walking up to the second floor; what really felt like lead was his mood—his feet feeling like lead was just a metaphor. It meant that he was starting to have second thoughts about this.

In contrast, Miyuki's footsteps were light. He didn't venture to ask why. He was at least smart enough to know what *she* was enjoying.

They headed for the end of the fourth-story hallway.

The door there was made of plywood and looked the same as the other classrooms. The differences amounted to a wood-carved plate buried in the middle, an intercom on the wall, and numerous security devices likely skillfully camouflaged.

The plate read STUDENT COUNCIL ROOM.

Miyuki was the one who had been invited—Tatsuya was just an extra. He yielded the duty of knocking to Miyuki. (Of course, only in a figurative sense. There wasn't actually a knocker on the door, just an intercom.)

Miyuki gracefully asked to be let in, and a bright word of welcome returned from the intercom speaker.

There was a soft sound of the door unlocking, so quiet that you wouldn't notice unless you strained your ears. Tatsuya placed his fingers on the door handle. Angling his body to be in front of his sister, he opened the door.

He knew that there wasn't any particular reason he needed to be cautious...but this was a habit that was part of them at this point.

"Welcome! Don't be shy—come on in." A voice addressed them from directly ahead, at the desk in the back.

Mayumi smiled, and Tatsuya found himself wanting to ask what on earth she was enjoying so much. She beckoned to them with her hand.

Miyuki passed in front, and Tatsuya followed behind. He stopped one pace in front of the door, and Miyuki two. She placed her hands together and looked down, giving a perfect bow that you could put in a textbook.

Tatsuya couldn't emulate such a refined act. The way she spoke and acted had been instilled in her by their late mother, someone Tatsuya hadn't had much contact with.

"Umm... How very polite of you."

At the sight of a bow that could get her into a party in the Imperial Palace, Mayumi seemed to falter a bit as well.

There were two other officers seated, but they were engrossed in

her aura. A third, the only nonofficer seated, the disciplinary committee president, maintained a calm expression, but Tatsuya got the
impression she was forcing herself a little to put on a poker face.

My sister seems like she's really going for this, he thought. However, he
didn't know exactly why Miyuki had done something so intimidating.

"Please, sit down. We can talk while we eat."

As if her pace had been ruined by Miyuki's preemptive strike, a
shadow crossed over Mayumi's tone of voice, which was casual at best
and overfamiliar at worst.

She was probably pointing out the long meeting table. The fact
that there were no information terminals embedded in it in this age
was probably in anticipation of its being used for food and drink.

In any case, she pulled out a chair and had Miyuki sit down at the
table, a thick wooden one unusual to see used as school equipment.
Tatsuya took a seat next to her, farther from the head of the table. His
sister would always stubbornly make him sit farther up the table from
her, but she understood that she was the guest of honor today, so she
seemed to be enduring it.

"Would you like meat, fish, or vegetarian?"

Astonishingly, not only was there a waiting machine—it had
multiple meal options. Tatsuya chose the vegetarian meal, and Miyuki
the same. One of the sophomores—if he recalled correctly, she was
Azusa Nakajou, the secretary—began to manipulate the machine,
which was positioned along the wall, and which was about the size of
a chest of drawers.

Now they only had to wait.

Mayumi sat at the head of the table; next to her, across from
Miyuki, was a female senior; next to her, across from Tatsuya, was
the disciplinary committee chairman, and next to her was Azusa.
Mayumi, having regained most of her composure, broached the topic.

"We were introduced during the entrance ceremony, but just
in case, I'll introduce everyone again. To my left is the accountant,
Suzune Ichihara, also known as Rin."

"...Only the president may call me that." Her face was proper, though each part of her face had the impression of being harsh. She was tall, and her limbs were long. The word *beauty* would have been a better way to describe her appearance than *pretty*. She certainly looked more like a "Miss Suzune" than a "Rin," which came from a different reading of one of the characters in her name.

"And next to her—you know her, right? She's Mari Watanabe, the head of the disciplinary committee."

This wasn't really a conversation, but nobody seemed to care. Maybe that meant that this was what usually happened.

"And then the secretary, Azusa Nakajou, also known as Ah-chan."

"President... Please, stop calling me Ah-chan in front of under-classmen. I have a position to think of, too, you know."

She was even smaller than Mayumi and had a baby face. Even if she didn't intend for her upturned eyes to look pouty, she still looked like a child about to cry.

I see. That must be "Ah-chan," thought Tatsuya. *That's unfortunate.*

"These members, with the addition of the vice president Hanzou, are the student council members this year."

"Except me, anyway."

"Right. Mari isn't with us. Oh, looks like it's finished!"

The panel on the dining server opened, and the meals came out on trays. The food lacked individuality, but they were all served correctly. There were five in total.

One's missing..., thought Tatsuya. It wasn't his place to speak, so as he wondered what to do, he saw Mari patiently take out a bento box.

Miyuki, seeing Azusa stand, also left her seat. The automatic waiting machine had, as its name implied, a function to automatically serve people, but if you didn't have a table specifically for it, it was faster to use human hands.

Azusa placed hers on the table first, then took Mayumi's and Suzune's in her hands. Then Miyuki carried hers and Tatsuya's to their seats, and the strange meal together began.

They started off with a harmless topic.

Although, among Tatsuya and Miyuki and the rest of them, there were basically no common topics. The conversation naturally drifted to the food they were currently eating.

There was no helping the fact that they were ready-made meals, since they were automatically cooked, but recent processed food was not all that inferior to normal cooking, though that was compared to average cooking. They couldn't deny that it was missing something.

"Did you make that bento yourself, Watanabe?" Miyuki's intent behind that question was simply to facilitate conversation; she didn't mean anything in particular by it.

"Yeah," nodded Mari. "...Is that strange?" She responded with her own hard-to-answer question in a voice that sounded a little deliberately mean. She wasn't saying it with any *actual* nastiness—she was only teasing her underclassman, since she appeared to be such a proper person.

"No, not at all," objected Tatsuya without skipping a beat before she could make Miyuki confused.

"...I see."

Tatsuya's eyes were on Mari's hands—more precisely, her fingers. Did she use a machine? Did she make it herself? How good was she at cooking? How bad was she...? Mari felt like he was seeing through all of it, and she was embarrassed.

"Perhaps we shall pack our own lunches beginning tomorrow as well."

Tatsuya naturally averted his gaze at Miyuki's casual remark. "Any bento you would make would be a very attractive prospect, but we don't have a place to eat..."

"Ah, that's right... We need to figure that out first..."

Their conversation—not the words being exchanged themselves, but rather the air between them as they spoke—seemed a little too friendly for family members of their age of opposite sex.

"...It's like a conversation between lovers."

Suzune dropped that bombshell without smiling an inch.

"Is that so? I would consider being her lover were we not blood related, but..." But Tatsuya replied in jest, and the bombshell failed to explode.

Or perhaps the bombshell was dropped on someone else—Azusa's face was flushed red in seriousness. "...I'm joking, of course," he declared flatly, without smiling an inch. There was no trace of panic in his words.

"You're not much fun, you know," evaluated Mari cheerlessly.

"I'm aware of that," responded Tatsuya in monotone.

"All right, all right, let's stop, Mari. I understand it's frustrating, but it seems that normal methods won't work on Tatsuya," interrupted Mayumi with a wry smile, having seen that there would be no end to it if she didn't.

"...You're right. I take back what I said. You're pretty interesting, Tatsuya."

She grinned—it was a handsome grin, despite her being a pretty female student—and overturned her appraisal. First the president, and now the disciplinary committee chairman.

It seemed he would get used to being called by his first name whether he liked it or not.

"Let's get to what we're here for, shall we?"

It felt a little sudden, but it wasn't as though high school lunch break was very long. They were already finished eating, too. Tatsuya and Miyuki both nodded at Mayumi's words, which had returned to their formal tone.

"Our school believes that student autonomy is important, and the student council is given broad authority within school. This is a general trend among public high schools, not only this school."

Tatsuya nodded to let her know he was listening. Control and autonomy were like waves breaking on the shore and retreating—their size differences tended to change in accordance with each other. After the complete victory at the Battle of Okinawa three years ago and the elevation of Japan's voice in the international arena, the nation saw a recoil away from the excessive importance placed on central control. It reflected unrest in internal affairs, stemming from the fact that the country's diplomatic environment had always been inferior. Society then swayed to place heavy emphasis on autonomy. And as backlash for *that*, certain private schools that still had strict management systems were gathering popularity from parents. The world couldn't be measured so simply.

"The student council here—traditionally, rights are collected on the student council president. You could call it a heavy concentration of power on that person."

Feeling uneasy at that statement was probably rude to Mayumi. Tatsuya drew back the reins on his mind.

"The student council president is chosen by election, but the president chooses the other student council members. Relieving members from their posts is also something entrusted only to the student council president. In all other committees, save for a few, the chairman has the right to appoint and dismiss members."

"The disciplinary committee I lead is one of those exceptions. The student council, the club committee, and the teachers' association elect three disciplinary committee members at a time through mutual election."

"So Mari, in a sense, has the same level of authority as me. Now, under this system, there is a limit to the term of office of the student president but not for the other members. The president's term in office is from the first of October to the thirtieth of September of the following year. During this time, the president can freely appoint and dismiss members."

He was starting to figure out where this was going, but he didn't interrupt. Instead, he nodded again to show his understanding.

"The usual custom is to make the freshman representative of the new students a member of the student council. The goal is to train a successor. Not all freshmen who become officers this way are chosen by the student council president, but that is how it has been for the past five years."

"So you were the head of the students when you enrolled, too? I should have known."

"Ah, well, that's right!" she stammered, her eyes wandering and her cheeks flushing ever so slightly,

Tatsuya's question had been a sort of flattery. He knew the answer when he asked it, but despite likely being used to hearing it, Mayumi looked honestly bashful. The fact that she was blushing for real, perhaps, meant that she wasn't *that* sophisticated...and she looked, at best, like someone the same age as him. —But maybe coming off as seriously embarrassed at just this was in itself an act.

"Ahem... Miyuki, I hereby request that you join the student council."

"Joining the student council," in this case, of course meant becoming a student council officer.

"Will you accept?"

There was a short pause as Miyuki's gaze lowered to her hands. She turned around to Tatsuya and silently asked him. Tatsuya gave her a small nod, full of encouragement. She looked down again, but when her head came back up, her eyes were worried for some reason.

"President, are you aware of my brother's grades?"

"—?" Tatsuya very nearly cried out at the entirely unexpected development. *What is she thinking, bringing that up so suddenly?*

"Yes, I am indeed. They are incredible... Frankly speaking, when a teacher showed me his answers in private, I lost a little confidence in myself."

"If you're going to let in high-achieving, efficient individuals, then I believe my brother would be a better choice than me."

"Hey, Mi—"

"If it's just desk work, then I don't think practical skill grades have anything to do with it. In fact, knowledge and judgment should be more important."

Miyuki almost *never* refuted something another person was saying with her own remarks. And she had done so even less with Tatsuya.

"I am greatly honored by your wish that I join the student council. I would very much like to be part of it, but is there no way my brother could come with me?"

Tatsuya covered his face. He wanted to look up and groan. Had he had such a negative influence on his sister? She must have known that taking a nepotistic attitude like this would only invite unease, so why?

Her action was not merely blind—it was a premeditated crime.

"Unfortunately, we cannot do that."

The answer came not from the president but from the seat next to her.

"The student council officers are selected from among the Course 1 students. This isn't an unwritten rule—it's an official regulation. It is the sole restriction placed upon the appointing and dismissing powers given to the president. This regulation was decided upon when the student council system became how it is now, and to overturn it we would need to have every student agree on a revision to the limitations of the student council. Two-thirds of the student body need to vote in agreement for it to go through, so with the Course 1 and Course 2 students being essentially equivalent in number, modifying the system is realistically impossible," declared Suzune dispassionately—or, if anything, remorsefully.

It was easy to understand from her tone that she, too, held a negative attitude toward the current system that discriminated between the Course 1 and Course 2 students as Blooms and Weeds.

"...I apologize. Please forgive my speaking out of place."

That was probably why Miyuki was able to apologize honestly, as well. Nobody was about to reproach her as she stood and bowed her head.

"Umm, well then, will you accept a position as secretary for this year's student council, Miyuki?"

"Yes, I will work my hardest. I look forward to working with you all."

Miyuki bowed again, though in a slightly more reserved manner this time, and Mayumi nodded with a satisfied smile.

"Please go ahead and ask Ah-chan about what your job actually entails."

"President, I said…to stop calling me Ah-chan—"

"If you have nothing else to do, would you be able to begin coming starting today after school?"

Not even paying attention to her baleful protest, Mayumi continued the conversation at her own pace.

"Miyuki." His sister had glanced back at him, but before she could say anything, Tatsuya said this short word with a slightly strong emphasis, recommending that she assent.

Miyuki's eyes showed agreement, and she turned back to face Mayumi. "I understand. I should come here after school, then, correct?"

"Yes. I'll be waiting for you, Miyuki."

"Excuse me… How come you call me Ah-chan, and just call her Miyuki…?"

It was a natural question, but again, she was ignored.

…Tatsuya started to feel sorry for Azusa.

"…There's a little longer until lunch break is over. Can I have a moment?"

Of course, it was also the fault of Mari stealing everyone's attention by raising her hand abruptly, though not in a bullying or teasing way to her.

"The student council's nomination for the disciplinary committee still hasn't been decided for the last empty spot created by last year's graduates."

"Didn't I say I was still in the process of selecting one? Not even a week has passed since the current year started. Don't rush me, Mari!" Mayumi discontentedly chided Mari on her impatience, but Mari didn't respond to it.

"If I'm correct, the stipulation for selecting student council officers said that, aside from the student president, you must appoint Course 1 students."

"That's right." *Unfortunate though it may be*, said her face as she nodded.

"The Course 1 restriction is only for the vice president, secretary, and accountant, correct?"

"Yes. The officers that make up the council are the president, vice president, secretary, and accountant, after all."

"So that means if the student council's appointee for the disciplinary committee was a student from Course 2, it wouldn't be against regulation."

"Mari, you…" Mayumi's eyes opened wide, and Suzune and Azusa made dumbfounded faces as well.

This proposition seemed to be just as tremendous as Miyuki's earlier remarks. *This Mari Watanabe seems to enjoy practical jokes a whole lot*, thought Tatsuya.

—However.

"Nice!"

"Huh?" Mayumi's unexpected cheer caused a stupid groan to escape him.

"That's right! There's no problem if it's the disciplinary committee, is there? Mari, the student council names Tatsuya Shiba to the disciplinary committee."

And all of a sudden, the situation had changed into something totally different.

"Wait a moment, please! What about my thoughts on this? I haven't even gotten a clear explanation of what a disciplinary committee member does." Tatsuya raised his voice in protest, more out of his danger sense going off than based on logical thought processes.

"Your sister hasn't received a concrete explanation of her job in the student council yet either, has she?" Suzune suddenly took the wind out of *that* sail, though.

"…Well, that's true, but…"

"Now, now, Rin, it's all right. Tatsuya, a disciplinary committee member is a person who maintains discipline in school."

"……"

"……"

"...Is that all?"

"That may not sound like very much, but it's a pretty tough...er, I mean, rewarding job!"

For now, he ignored the part Mayumi smiled past and rephrased. There was a more fundamental discrepancy in their mutual understanding.

"That isn't what I meant..."

"What?"

Mayumi didn't *seem* to be playing dumb. Tatsuya slid his gaze to the right.

Suzune's eyes were sympathetic. But she wasn't about to throw him a lifeboat.

Next to her—Mari looked amused.

Next to her—when their eyes met, panic entered Azusa's face.

He stared. He peered into her eyes, which were bouncing and wandering left and right.

"Umm, our disciplinary committee is an organization that manages people who violate school regulations."

—She was as timid as her appearance suggested.

"It's called the disciplinary committee, but things like dress code violations and being late are handled by a weekly autonomous committee."

This student council having "personality" was an understatement—would she really be able to survive in a place like this? Self-induced though it was, Tatsuya began to worry.

"...Umm, did you have a question?"

"No, please continue."

"Um, yes. The disciplinary committee's main responsibility is to expose those who violate school regulations by using magic, and to control disturbances where magic is used.

"The head of the disciplinary committee gets the final say in the offender's punishment, and along with the student council president, who acts as representative of the student body, attends the disciplinary meeting and can offer her own opinions. In other words, it's a combination between the police and the prosecutor."

"But that's amazing, Tatsuya!" said Miyuki.

"Come on, Miyuki... Wait a moment before giving me those 'it's decided!' eyes... I just want to make sure of something." Instead of turning to Azusa, who had been explaining, he turned to Mari.

"What?"

"By that explanation, the disciplinary committee members need to stop fights by force if they happen, right?"

"That's about right. Even if magic isn't being used, that's our duty."

"And when magic is used, we need to stop it."

"Before it's used at all, ideally."

"Excuse me! I'm a Course 2 student because my practical skill grades were poor!" Tatsuya finally raised his voice. It sounded like you needed enough power to hold down an opponent with magic to do this job. However he thought about it, it wasn't a role they should be giving to a Course 2 student with inferior magical abilities.

However, the reprimanded Mari readily gave a too-simple answer with a cool face. "That's okay."

"What is?!"

"If it's a contest of strength, then we have me... Whoops, looks like lunch is just about over. I'd like to continue this after school— would you mind?"

Lunch break was certainly almost over, and the conversation was certainly not one to be left at vagaries.

"...All right."

Agreeing to show up here a second time made him feel like this situation was inevitable, like his outer moat and inner moat had already been breached, but Tatsuya didn't have any other options.

"Okay, then come here later."

Tatsuya stifled his feeling of how unreasonable this was and nodded. Miyuki, while still considerate of her brother's feelings, couldn't hide her own happiness.

◇ ◇ ◇

Thanks to the proliferation of educational terminals, a theory was once popular that school was unnecessary. It supposed that because you can have class over a network, taking such long trips to and from a school was a waste of time and energy.

In the end, this "unnecessary school theory" never evolved out of a fad. However far interfaces advanced technologically, virtual experiences would never be reality. For things like practice and experimentation, sufficient learning effects couldn't be gained unless it was a real-life experience accompanied by real-time question-and-answer sessions—and there was learning promotion effect in learning in a group with others of the same age. These two points had been proven by trial and error using human experiment-like trials.

Class 1-E was currently right smack in the middle of one of those practicum classes.

That said, there was no teacher present for the real-time question-and-answer session. It was an easily understood example that the fruits of academic research weren't necessarily adopted logically.

The students of 1-E were following the control procedure displayed on the wall monitor and manipulating the stationary educational CAD. Today's class was a primer to a primer—learning how to control this machine used in class.

It was real-life guidance, but there was still a task to perform. There was no teacher overseeing them, so submitting a task was the only standard of this course. Today's task was to use this CAD to make a small push car about thirty centimeters long move from one end of a rail to another, then back, three times over.

Without actually touching the push car, of course.

"Tatsuya, how was it in the student council room?"

As Tatsuya was standing in line waiting to use the CAD, no sooner had he been poked in the back than Leo shot him a question. His face didn't seem to be hiding anything, so he must have just had a keen interest.

"It got a little weird..."

"Weird how?" Erika, who was in front of Tatsuya, spun around and tilted her head.

"They told me to be on the disciplinary committee. It was so sudden. I wonder what that was all about." Tatsuya, too, tilted his head in thought. *What was that about?* was really the only thing he felt like he could say about it.

"Yeah, that is pretty sudden." Leo seemed to feel the abruptness as well.

"But isn't that pretty impressive? You got scouted by the student council!"

Mizuki, however, seemed to feel differently. She had stopped on her way back to the end of the line to rechallenge the task (not that she had failed or anything) and was looking at Tatsuya with admiration. The lines to the left and right of them getting a little noisy was probably because his other classmates felt the same way as Mizuki.

But Tatsuya couldn't honestly accept Mizuki's words of praise. "Is it? I was just along with my sister."

Erika gave a small, wry smile at Tatsuya's stubbornly skeptical attitude. "Oh, don't be so mean to yourself. What does the disciplinary committee do, anyway?" she asked. Tatsuya explained in summary what Azusa had told him, and the three's eyes went wide.

"That definitely seems like a troublesome job..." Leo sighed; beside him, Mizuki flip-flopped and gave a worried expression.

"Isn't that dangerous, though...? Erika, what's wrong?"

Erika looked displeased—actually, she looked angry for some reason. "...God, so selfish..." Her gaze was strangely averted. Her words, spoken while glaring at empty space—were they rebuking someone not here?

"Erika?" repeated Mizuki.

"Eh? Ah, I'm sorry. What a terrible story. Tatsuya, it's dangerous. Just turn it down!" Erika tempted in a purposefully bright voice, her stern expression giving way to a mischievous smile.

"Huh? No, it sounds fun! You should do it, Tatsuya. I'll root for you!"

Tatsuya knew she was trying to cover something up with a joking tone, but what was she trying to cover up?

"But if you have to mediate in fights, you could get mixed up in some attack magic, right?" asked Mizuki.

Now he thought he knew who she was referring to when she said "selfish."

"Yeah. And there will probably be guys who would hate you for no reason because of it, too."

But the atmosphere wasn't right for him to get more information from Erika.

"But don't you think Tatsuya would be better than some over-bearing Course 1 kid walking up uninvited?"

And he had no intention of barging in on the conversation with the question.

"Hmm… You might be right."

"Erika, don't be so easily convinced! If that's the case, he just shouldn't get into fights, right?"

"But, Mizuki, even if we don't intend to, sometimes you have to put out the fires before they start, right? Like what happened yesterday."

Mizuki groaned. "That was—"

"People get away with false accusations and charges all the time. It's the world we live in."

In fact, the winds had started blowing in a bad direction, making Tatsuya feel the need to block it off. "Hey, Erika, it's your turn."

"Ack, sorry, sorry!"

Urged on by Tatsuya, Erika, panicking a bit, took her position. He could tell just by looking at her back that she was giving it her all. She didn't seem at all like the idle chat had dragged her down. She appeared to be the type of person who could switch her brain quickly from one thing to the next. Frivolous though she might seem, perhaps she was actually serious at heart.

Erika's back moved up and down slightly—she was probably taking a breath.

After a pause, he "saw" the psionic waves—a form of light invisible to the naked eye, but detectable by magicians—from behind her. It was the light of the extra psions not used for the activation program deployment or the execution of the magic program that followed. There wasn't as little excess psionic light as a well-finessed magician, but for a freshman in high school, it was pretty high level. When the excess light reached a certain level, it would be accompanied by a physical luminescence because of photon interference, but perhaps the fact that it didn't happen that way meant that she had it well under control.

The cart placed in front of the CAD began to run, then looped back again. It repeated the process three times. She must have been satisfied with the result herself—Tatsuya could see her making a furtive fist with her right hand as if to say, *Nice!* The cart was certainly moving more briskly than in the previous practice session. Specifically its acceleration and deceleration both were quick.

For this practice, you accelerated the cart to the halfway point on the rail, then decelerated it to a stop at the end, then accelerated and decelerated in the other direction, making three full round trips. The activation programs registered in the CAD were magic program "blueprints" implementing six acceleration/deceleration technique sets. There was no designation for how great the acceleration should be, so that part of it ended up reflecting the student's capacity. The fact that the cart had moved energetically meant that her magic had been that good.

Erika went around to the back of her line with an unconcerned face—you couldn't tell at all that she had just done a secret fist pump. To replace her, Tatsuya stepped up to the stationary CAD.

He adjusted the height of the legs supporting the CAD with a pedal, then pressed the palm of his hand against the translucent white panel covering the entire surface of its housing, which was about the size of a filing cabinet, and began to circulate psions.

Resisting the urge to grimace at the noise feedback in the activation program, he constructed a magic program.

After appearing to stumble two or three times, the push car safely began to move.

Today's practicum was purely to get the students used to the CAD they'd be using in class—time wasn't being kept. But that was something that nobody but Tatsuya himself was aware of.

The time it took to get the push car moving was clearly longer than when Erika did it. No, not only Erika. It might be faster to count *up* from the bottom of the twenty-five students in 1-E.

The energy of the push car itself didn't unfavorably compare to the other students. So it didn't stand out in particular.

But Tatsuya himself was acutely aware of the results, and it made him want to heave a sigh.

◇ ◇ ◇

He was grateful they hadn't been envious or jealous of him, but being sent off with a hearty "Good luck!" sort of ruined the mood—it would just bring his spirits down instead. It was all the more difficult, because Tatsuya himself didn't have any enthusiasm in the first place.

After school, he trudged to the student council room, his feet even heavier than they had been during lunch.

Atmosphere-wise it was a slightly miserable composition, but Miyuki held her tongue out of understanding for his warped sentiments.

Their ID cards had already been registered with the authentication system (he was opposed to already considering himself to have entered the disciplinary committee, but Mayumi and Mari had both had their own way with him), so they entered without incident.

He was greeted by a sharp gaze teeming with distinct hostility.

The origin was on the other side of the workstation console buried in the wall. Sitting in the seat that had been empty during lunch.

"Excuse us."

Again, he couldn't brag about it, but Tatsuya was used to this type of look and atmosphere. *Is that sad?* When he maintained his poker face and bowed slightly without a word, the hostility dispersed as though it had never been there. Although it wasn't as if the hostility toward him had disappeared—it had just shifted to interest in Miyuki, who had taken her place standing in front of him, and nobody needed to explain *that* to him.

The glare's owner rose and approached the siblings. No—maybe it was more accurate to say that he approached Miyuki. Tatsuya recalled his face. He was the second-year student who'd sat right behind Mayumi during the entrance ceremony—which meant he was the vice president of the student council.

His height was about the same as Tatsuya's. His breadth was a little on the thin side.

He was put together, but his features bore no special mention, and his physique was nothing particularly special. He didn't give an impression of being very physically strong, but the radiance of the psions encroaching upon the surrounding air spoke to the young man's excelling magical power.

"I am the vice president, Gyoubu Hattori. Miyuki Shiba, welcome to the student council." His voice seemed a little wound up, but considering his age, he was exhibiting enough self-control. His right hand twitched— perhaps because he considered shaking hands, then stopped himself.

Tatsuya didn't have the mind to inquire why he stopped.

Hattori returned to his seat after that, completely ignoring Tatsuya. He felt a hint of indignation from behind Miyuki, but it disappeared instantly. Nobody other than Tatsuya, who was standing right behind her, would have noticed it. Tatsuya privately put his hand to his chest, relieved she had managed to control herself.

Without a care to his anxiety—though considering that they were strangers he just met, there was no helping that—they were welcomed by two casual greetings, without touching on the vice president's action, which had caused it.

"Hey, you're here."

"Welcome, Miyuki. And thank you for coming as well, Tatsuya."

The one who lightly waved to him and who was already treating him like a friend was Mari, and the one who naturally treated him differently was Mayumi. Of course, neither of those things exactly got on his nerves.

Tatsuya had already arrived in the state of mind that said worrying about these two wouldn't get him anywhere.

"Sorry to get right to it, but Ah-chan, could you...?"

"...All right."

Her state of mind was one of resignation as well. Azusa cast down her eyes in sadness for a moment, then smiled awkwardly and nodded. She guided Miyuki over to the terminal on the wall.

"Okay, we should get moving, too."

He felt like her tone of voice had changed quite a bit in just one day, but Tatsuya figured that was probably because this casual way of speaking was more Mari's thing.

"To where?"

Tatsuya, however, hadn't been given a royal upbringing, and didn't care how she talked. He simply responded to what he was told.

"The disciplinary committee HQ. I figure it'll be easier to have you see everything. It's the room right under this. Oh, but it's connected in the middle."

Tatsuya paused before replying to Mari's answer. "...That's an odd structure."

"I agree," she said, rising from her seat. However, before she got all the way up, she was stopped.

"Please wait, Watanabe."

The one who stopped her was Vice President Hattori. Mari responded to him using a name he wasn't yet familiar with.

"What's up, Vice President Hanzou Gyoubu-Shoujou Hattori?"

"Please don't call me by my full name!"

Tatsuya unthinkingly glanced at Mayumi. She bent her head a bit, wondering why he did so. *I never thought "Hanzou" was his real name... It was completely unexpected.*

"Okay, then Vice President Hanzou Hattori."

"It's Gyoubu Hattori!"

"That's not your name; it's just your official position. In your family."

Indeed, the term *gyoubu-shoujou* referred to a junior to the traditional "minister of justice" position in premodern Japan.

"I have no rank right now. The school has accepted my registered name of Gyoubu Hattori! ...But that isn't what I wanted to say!"

"You were the one hung up on it."

"Now, Mari, there are some things that Hanzou won't give ground on," remarked Mayumi.

Everyone turned to glare at her, as if to say, *You're not one to talk.*

But she showed no signs of responding to them.

Maybe she didn't even realize it.

And for some reason, Hattori didn't say anything, either. But it wasn't quite like he didn't know how to deal with her—Tatsuya got a glimpse of a different sort of emotion than the one he'd had with Mari, and it was quite interesting to him.

——Insofar as he was a third-party witness to it, anyway.

But he couldn't remain a spectator for more than a few moments. "Watanabe, what I wanted to talk about was the disciplinary committee replacement."

The blood that had risen to his face all receded. Hattori regained his composure as if this were a time-lapse video.

"What?"

"I'm opposed to naming that freshman a member of the committee," opined Hattori calmly—perhaps suppressing his emotion.

Mari frowning at that didn't seem to be an act, necessarily. He couldn't tell whether her expression was one of surprise, one of being fed up with him, or what emotion she had, though. "Don't be silly. President Saegusa is the one who nominated Tatsuya Shiba as the student council's selection. Even if it was an oral nomination, it doesn't change the effectiveness of the nomination."

"I heard he hasn't accepted yet. It isn't an official nomination until the person accepts it."

"That would be Tatsuya's problem. The student council's opinion has already been articulated by the student council president. The decision is for him to make, not you," said Mari, looking between Tatsuya and Hattori.

Hattori didn't spare a glance for Tatsuya. He was purposely ignoring him.

Suzune looked at the two of them calmly, Azusa in a fluster, and Mayumi with an unreadable, archaic smile. Miyuki was meekly keeping herself by the wall. However, Tatsuya was on edge, though in a different way from Azusa—he didn't know when his sister might spontaneously discharge again.

"There is no precedent for nominating a Weed to the disciplinary committee."

The epithet in Hattori's response raised Mari's eyebrows slightly. "That's a prohibited word, Vice President Hattori. The disciplinary committee has decided that it's a discriminatory term. You've got some balls using it right in front of the committee's leader."

Hattori didn't appear frightened by her words, which could be taken either as a reprimand or a warning, or both.

"There's no point in keeping up appearances, is there? Or do you plan to reprimand more than a third of all the students in this school? The distinction between Blooms and Weeds is recognized by the school and built into the school system. And there's enough of a gap in skill between them to form the foundation for that distinction. Members of the disciplinary committee are tasked with using real ability to crack down on students who don't follow the rules. A Weed's real ability is inferior, and thus they cannot serve in it."

Mari answered Hattori's arrogant declaration with a cold smile. "The disciplinary committee does see real ability as more important, but there are many kinds of ability. If we just need someone to be *overpowering*, we have me. Whether I'm against ten people or twenty, I can deal with them all myself. The only ones who can fight on an even level with me are President Saegusa and Chairman Juumonji, after all. By your logic, we wouldn't need talented people lacking in real combat abilities. Or do you want to fight me, Vice President Hattori?"

Mari's words had confidence and results backing them up. But though Hattori winced and lost the mental battle against her, he didn't seem to have any intention of raising the white flag. "I'm not making myself the problem. It's a matter of his aptitude."

Of course, Hattori firmly believed what he was saying was correct. Less powerful Course 2 students couldn't be part of the disciplinary committee, since it demanded the use of force. That fact was proven by the reality that no Course 2 student had ever been chosen for the disciplinary committee.

But Mari's own confidence was stronger than his. "Didn't I just say there's more than one kind of ability? Tatsuya has the eyes and mind to read into activation programs as they're expanding and predict the magic they're executing."

"…What?" asked Hattori reflexively—he hadn't expected those words. Maybe he didn't believe what he'd heard.

Reading into activation programs. There was no way someone could do that. That was common sense to him.

"What I'm saying is he can tell what kind of magic someone was trying to use even if they didn't actually activate it." But Mari's answer didn't change. She spoke without uncertainty that it was the truth and that it was possible.

"The rules of punishment of our school vary based on the variety and scale of the magic the person tried to use. But if you do like

Mayumi does and destroy the activation program before the magic program goes off, we won't know what kind of magic they were trying to use. But if we let the activation program expand, we're putting the cart before the horse. If you can cancel the activation expand while it's in the deployment stage, it's safer that way. We've always had trouble deciding how to punish attempted criminals, and we sometimes have to let them off easy. He'll be a huge help in that regard."

"...But would he be able to stop the magic from executing at the scene of an actual crime...?" His tone couldn't conceal his shock, and Hattori attempted to somehow argue against her.

"That goes for Course 1 freshmen, too. Even for sophomores—how many people do you think have the skills to stop an opponent's magic from activating by using your own after they start?" Mari flat-out rejected what he said, but that wasn't all. "And besides, there's one other reason I want him on the committee."

Even Hattori couldn't immediately find any words to respond with.

"Until now, no Course 2 students have been nominated for the disciplinary committee. In other words, Course 1 students have been in control of magic-related offenses committed by Course 2 students. Like you said, there's an emotional gap between the Course 1 and Course 2 students here. The system of Course 1 kids controlling Course 2 kids and not the other way around is making it worse. As head of the committee, I would prefer not to do anything that would promote this attitude of discrimination."

"Wow... That's amazing, Mari. You thought of all that yourself? I completely thought you just liked Tatsuya."

"President, please."

Mayumi nearly shattered the mood, but Suzune held her in check.

One bore a reproachful look.

The other shook her head.

The first was Mayumi, and the second Suzune.

The emotional confrontation, still not yet decided, continued to spew its toxins.

"President… As the vice president, I oppose Tatsuya Shiba's election to the disciplinary committee. I admit that Chairman Watanabe has a point, but I still believe that the disciplinary committee's original goal is to suppress and expose violations of school rules. A Course 2 student lacking in magic ability isn't fit for the post. Your mistaken appointment of him will surely come back to hurt your credibility in the end. I urge you to reconsider."

"Wait, please!"

Tatsuya panicked and turned around. As he had feared, Miyuki had finally lost her patience. He had been too caught up in Mari's speech to time controlling her properly. He hurriedly attempted to stop her, but Miyuki had already begun to speak.

"This may sound forward, Vice President. My brother's grades in practical magic may not be sterling, but that's only because the way they evaluate the practicum test doesn't match up with his strengths. When it comes to real combat, nobody can beat him."

Her words were filled with confidence, and Mari lightly opened her eyes wider. Mayumi's vague smile went away, too, and she gave Miyuki and Tatsuya a serious look. But there wasn't very much seriousness in Hattori's stare back.

"Shiba…" Hattori was, of course, talking to Miyuki. "Magicians must be able to think calmly and logically and take everything in stride. Partiality toward one's family members may be inevitable for normal people, but as people aiming to be magicians, we cannot allow our eyes to be clouded by nepotism. Please take that to heart."

He sounded like a relative showing her the way—he didn't seem to mean anything by it. He was probably just trying to be an excellent upperclassman who looked out for other Course 1 students, if a little self-righteously. —In this case, though, it seemed evident ever since Miyuki began to argue that his way of speaking would have the opposite effect.

As expected, Miyuki grew more riled up. "A word, if I may—my eyes are not clouded! If we just look at my brother's real power—"

III

"Miyuki!" He held his hands aloft before Miyuki, who was on the verge of completely losing her cool. She looked taken aback, then, in shame and regret, closed her mouth and looked down.

Tatsuya, who had stopped his sister with words and gestures, moved in front of Hattori.

Miyuki had definitely said too much. She even nearly said something she never should have. But Hattori was the one who made her go that far. Tatsuya had no mind to make Miyuki to be the only bad guy here.

"Vice President Hattori, would you like to have a mock duel with me?"

"What…?"

Hattori, the challenged, wasn't the only one struck dumb by the unexpected proposal. Mayumi and Mari were also staring hard at the two of them, astonished at his bold, unpredicted counterattack.

With the stares of everyone in the room on them, Hattori's body began to tremble. "Don't get ahead of yourself, you *substitute!*"

Someone yelped—was it Azusa? The other three, as might be expected of upperclassmen, were keeping their calm. And as for the one on the receiving end of the insult, he was making a troubled sort of face, giving a faint, wry grin.

"What's so funny?!"

"Shouldn't magicians always keep their calm?"

"Pah!" Ridiculed by his own words, Hattori spat out a quick grunt of frustration.

Tatsuya's tongue didn't stop there. He didn't feel like stopping it. "I don't think you would understand my personal combat skills in practice unless you fought me. It's not as though I want to become a member of the disciplinary committee…but if it's to prove my sister's eyes aren't clouded, then I have no choice," he murmured, as though he were talking to itself.

That only made it sound unnecessarily provocative to Hattori. "…Fine by me. I'll teach you to respect your superiors."

He didn't let his agitation last for long—proof, perhaps, that he wasn't all bark. His controlled tone of voice instead spoke to the depth of his rage.

Mayumi spoke up without a moment's delay. "With the power invested in me as student council president, I hereby acknowledge the mock battle between Gyoubu Hattori of 2-B and Tatsuya Shiba of 1-E as an official duel."

"Based on the student council president's declaration, as the chairman of the disciplinary committee, I hereby acknowledge this duel to be an extracurricular activity grounded in school rules."

"It will be held thirty minutes from now in Seminar 3. The duel will be private. Both combatants are permitted to use CADs."

Mock battles were an act of violence, and prohibited by school rules—a measure to prevent things from escalating to fights.

After Mayumi and Mari solemnly stated that they didn't care, Azusa frantically began typing on her terminal.

◇ ◇ ◇

"Three days in, and the cat's out of the bag already..." Tatsuya grumbled in front of the door to Seminar 3. He had exchanged his license, stamped by the student president (these things were still made out of paper) for his CAD case.

He heard a near-crying voice from behind him. "I'm so sorry..."

"There's nothing for you to apologize about."

"But my actions have caused you trouble—"

He turned around, took half a step, and held his hand out to her head.

Miyuki gave a start, then closed her eyes. But at the sensation of him gently stroking her hair, she timidly brought her head up. Her eyes looked ready to burst forth with tears at any moment.

"I told you on the day of the entrance ceremony, remember? You always get angry in my place, since I can't. You're always saving me... So don't say you're sorry. There are different words for this situation."

"All right... Good luck," replied Miyuki, wiping her tears and smiling. Tatsuya smiled back with a nod and opened the door to the seminar room.

"I didn't expect that." As soon as he opened the door, he heard that phrase.

"Expect what?"

The one to welcome Tatsuya to the seminar room was Mari, who had been named as the referee.

"That you were the type who loves a good skirmish. I had you pegged for someone who didn't care about what other people said." Though she said it was unexpected, her eyes glittered in anticipation.

Tatsuya used his steely self-control—well, perhaps that's an exaggeration—to suffocate the deep sigh that had made its way into his throat.

"I thought it was the disciplinary committee's job to stop this sort of personal struggle." A somewhat sarcastic remark leaped out instead of the sigh, perhaps inevitably.

But Mari didn't seem to respond to it at all. "It's not personal. This is an official match. Mayumi said so, remember? We may look at your abilities first and foremost, but that policy doesn't just apply between Course 1 and Course 2 students—in fact we normally apply it to two Course 1 students. A Course 1 and Course 2 student using this method to settle something is probably a first, though."

I see. That means they're actually encouraging settling matters by force when they can't be solved through talking. "Did these 'official matches' become more frequent after you became the head of the disciplinary committee?"

"Yeah, they have been." Her completely frank response even made Miyuki, standing behind Tatsuya, grin drily. Then her expression suddenly got serious, and she brought her face toward his. "So are you confident?"

A whispered question, spoken so close he could hear her breathe. Miyuki's beautiful eyebrows shot up at her altogether too-close distance, but Tatsuya, whose vision was dominated by Mari's mean-ingful grin, fortunately (?) didn't notice his younger sister's excessive response. Mari's long, slitted eyes looking up at him from half a head below, and the faintly sweet aroma drifting to him—Tatsuya realized he was feeling sexually aroused.

The moment he realized it, the object of "himself" became a phe-nomenon born with him, and he cut it off. He converted his excite-ment into a simple stream of data.

"Hattori is one of the top five magic users in the school. He may be more suited for group combat than individual fights, but still, not many people can beat him one-on-one," whispered Mari in a glossy alto, yet without a hint of sex appeal.

"I don't plan on competing with him head-on." But Tatsuya answered her curtly and in a mechanical voice, without showing a hint of unrest.

"You're pretty calm… I've lost a little self-confidence," she replied, clearly amused.

"Huh." Tatsuya nodded vaguely, without trying to give a different response.

"If you were cute enough to blush at times like these, there would probably be more people willing to help you out, you know." She flashed him a grin and withdrew, making her way to the starting line in the middle.

"How annoying…" *She must be the type to demand chaos where there is order, and bring order where there is chaos*, thought Tatsuya. For those mak-ing peaceful livings, she was nothing but a troublemaker.

He breathed another sigh—this one at the remarkably troubling interpersonal relationships he'd made since enrolling here.

He opened his CAD case. Inside the black attaché case, there were two handgun-shaped CADs. He took one of them, unloaded the magazine, and switched it out for another.

Everyone but Miyuki watched him with deep fascination.

"Sorry for the wait."

"Do you always walk around with more than one like that?"

Specialized CADs were limited in the number of activation programs they could use. Multipurpose CADs could store ninety-nine activation programs, regardless of family. On the other hand, specialized CADs could store only a combination of nine activation programs belonging to the same family. A CAD was once developed to make it possible to swap out the activation programs recording storage mechanism to make up for this fault, but the specialized type was favored by magicians specializing in specific types of magic programs in the first place. There wasn't much need for an increase in magic variations. The majority of people would only end up using one type of magic even if they carried more than one piece of storage on them.

But Tatsuya's answer, given in response to Mari's obvious curiosity, displayed that he was part of the minority. "Yes. I don't have enough mental faculty to use a multipurpose type."

Hattori, standing in front of him, gave a derisive snort upon hearing that, but it didn't even make a ripple in Tatsuya's mind.

"All right, then I'll explain the rules. Any techniques that would result in the death of the opponent, whether direct or indirect attacks, are forbidden. Any techniques that would result in irreversible injury are forbidden. Techniques that directly damage the opponent's flesh are forbidden. However, direct attacks not resulting in more than a sprain are permitted. The usage of weapons is forbidden. Unarmed attacks are permitted. If you want to use kicking moves, take your shoes off now and exchange them for the school's padded shoes. The match is over when one side admits defeat or when a judge determines it's impossible to continue. You must back up to the starting positions and not activate your CAD until the signal is given. Not following these rules will result in an immediate loss—and I'll step in and stop you myself, so you'd better be prepared if you don't. That is all."

Tatsuya and Hattori both nodded, then faced each other from the starting lines, five meters apart. Neither of their expressions were tense, nor were they scornful or provoking. However, Tatsuya caught a glimpse of relaxation in Hattori's face. They were too far apart for either's hands to reach the other. Even with the momentum of a pro football player, using magic would be quicker at this distance.

Since this was a contest of magic, it was only natural that attacks using magic were established as advantageous. In this sort of duel, the one who hit with their magic first usually won. Even if they couldn't knock the opponent out with one hit, the opponent wouldn't avoid damage. There weren't many people possessed of the mental fortitude to calmly construct spells while taking damage from magic. As soon as you were hit by a magical attack, any magic you were in the middle of creating would fizzle. It would be over once your opponent pressed their attack.

And with the rule that they activated their CADs at the same time, Hattori had complete confidence that he, a Course 1 student, couldn't possibly lose to a pretentious new Course 2 student. The CAD was the fastest magic-activating tool. Even if you snuck in something other than a CAD before the signal to start was given, it wouldn't match the CAD's speed. And the speed of executing magic using the CAD was the greatest point of evaluation in terms of one's grades in practical magic. It could also be said equated to the greatest difference between Blooms and Weeds.

Tatsuya's CAD—a specialized type in the shape of a handgun.

Hattori's CAD—a multipurpose type in the orthodox bracelet form.

Specialized CADs excelled in speed, and multipurpose ones in versatility. However, even though specialized types won out in speed over multipurpose types, that wouldn't be enough to fill the gap between a Bloom and a Weed. That went double if the opponent was a new student.

Hattori considered that there were no factors that could defeat him—and that could be called neither hubris nor carelessness.

Tatsuya pointed his right hand, holding his CAD toward the floor...

...Hattori placed his right hand before the CAD on his left arm...

…and both waited for Mari's signal.

The room fell deathly silent.

And at the very moment silence had established complete dominance over them—

"Go!"

—the official duel between Tatsuya and Hattori commenced.

Hattori's right hand flew over his CAD.

Though he had to press only three simple keys, his motions were entirely without hesitation. The type of technique he originally specialized in was wide-scope attack magic for midrange and farther. In a close-range, one-on-one battle, he was comparatively worse.

But that was only *comparatively* so, and in the year since he had enrolled at First High, he was undefeated.

There were those he might yield to. Mari, who was a specialist in personal combat, whether against a single person or a group. Mayumi, who could freely use astoundingly swift and accurate gunning magic. Juumonji, the head of the club committee, nicknamed the Iron Wall. Aside from those three giants, he would boast that neither students *nor* teachers could outdo him.

That wasn't necessarily a subjective opinion.

Hattori immediately finished expanding a simple activation program—he had gone for speed—and in a flash, he began to execute his magic.

A moment later, he very nearly screamed.

His opponent in this match, this first-year kid who didn't know his place, had gotten so close that he was filling his vision.

He hastily corrected his coordinates and attempted to fire off the magic. It was movement magic, one of the fundamental families of magic. Hattori's magic program had locked on to his opponent, and it *should* have blown him over ten meters backward, the impact from which would have taken him out of the fight.

But his magic fizzled out.

It wasn't that he had failed to process the activation program.

His enemy had disappeared.

The coordinates used by magic programs didn't require much in the way of precision, but when the target in your vision suddenly disappears from it—and thus from your awareness—an error would occur no matter what. The psion information bodies that should have altered the target's state of movement dispersed without any effect.

Panicked, Hattori looked right and left. Then he was rocked by a violent "wave" from the side.

Three of them hit him in sequence.

Each separate wave overlapped inside his body, forming a giant undulation, and took his consciousness away.

The victor was decided in the blink of an eye.

The term *insta-kill* was extremely appropriate—the match hadn't lasted five seconds.

On the other end of Tatsuya's pointed CAD's muzzle was Hattori, collapsed in a heap.

"...The winner is Tatsuya Shiba." Mari was actually hesitant in announcing the result.

There was no joy on the victor's face. He looked like he had just done what he needed to, without any emotion.

He gave a light bow and headed for the desk his CAD case was on. He wasn't trying to strike a pose. It was clear he had no interest whatsoever in his victory.

"Wait," Mari called out to stop him from behind. "Those movements… Did you expand a self-accelerating technique beforehand?"

At her question, Mayumi, Suzune, and Azusa reflected on the duel they'd just seen. At the same time the signal for the duel came out, Tatsuya's body had moved right in front of Hattori. And in the next moment, his body was in a few meters to Hattori's right side. It was so fast it looked like teleportation—a movement a physical human body should have been incapable of making.

"I believe you're in the best position to know otherwise." But this was as Tatsuya said.

As the referee, Mari had been keenly watching for any false starts activating their CADs. She had also theorized the presence of another, hidden CAD in addition to the one she saw, and had closely observed the flow of psions.

"It's just that..."

"It wasn't magic. It was a physical technique, plain and simple."

"I can vouch for him. That's the martial art my brother uses. He receives guidance from a *ninjutsu* user named Yakumo Kokonoe."

Mari caught her breath.

She excelled in interpersonal combat, and she knew the name Yakumo Kokonoe quite well. Even Mayumi and Suzune, who didn't know of Yakumo as well as Mari did, couldn't conceal their surprise at how profound the old arts were, and how they allowed one to achieve movement on the level of magically assisted action using purely physical techniques.

Of course, they weren't only surprised.

Mayumi offered a new question, from the point of view of someone studying magic.

"Then was the magic you used to attack *ninjutsu* as well? All I could see was you looking like you fired a wave of just psions, and nothing else." Nevertheless, her voice and word choice were stiff and formal, possibly because of the amazement that she couldn't conceal.

It was bad manners for magicians to pry into how exclusive techniques used by other magicians worked. But Mayumi, who could easily fire psionic bullets as her own special magic, couldn't seem to suppress her interest in the mechanisms used by Tatsuya's attack, which appeared to have used psions—particles without a physical function—as a weapon, to damage Hattori.

"It isn't *ninjutsu*, but you're correct that it was a psionic wave. It was a basic vibration-type spell. I only made psionic waves."

"But that doesn't explain why Hanzou went down..."

"He got sick."

"Sick? From what, exactly?"

Taking care not to appear exasperated with the confused Mayumi, Tatsuya flatly continued his explanation. "Magicians can detect psions in the same way as visible light rays and audible sound waves. This is an indispensable skill for actually using magic. However, as a side effect, magicians exposed to unanticipated psionic waves actually feel like their bodies are jolting around. That was what he felt, and it had an effect on his physical body. It's the same mechanism as in hypnotism, where if you suggest a person got sunburned, actual blisters appear on them. In this case, because of that rocking sensation, he essentially came down with a bad case of seasickness."

"I don't believe it… Magicians are exposed to psionic waves all the time. He should be used to them. Typeless magic goes without saying, but even activation and magic programs are types of psionic waves. So how on earth did you create a wave strong enough to cause a *magician* to lose his footing…?"

The one to answer Mayumi's question was Suzune. "I see. Constructive interference."

"Rin?" Even the sagacious Mayumi couldn't understand what she meant from only that.

Of course, Suzune's explanation wasn't finished. "He created three psionic waves with different frequencies, set it up so that the three waves would combine right where Hattori was standing, and produced a strong, triangular wave. I'm impressed you can do such precise calculations."

"You're very perceptive, Ichihara."

Suzune was struck dumb by Tatsuya's calculation abilities, but Tatsuya thought to himself that *she* was more amazing for being able to realize that after seeing it only once.

But it seemed that Suzune's actual question led elsewhere. "Still, how did you activate three magic waves in such a short period of time? With that level of throughput, your practical evaluation shouldn't have been so low."

Tatsuya couldn't help but give a wry smile at being told outright that he had poor grades.

Instead, Azusa, who had been repeatedly glancing at Tatsuya's hands unsteadily for a while now, timidly suggested an answer. "Umm, could your CAD be the Silver Horn?"

"Silver Horn? Silver—you mean the mysterious, genius magic engineer, Taurus Silver?"

Asked by Mayumi, Azusa's expression immediately brightened. Azusa, sometimes teased as a "device nerd," merrily began to speak.

"That's right! The miraculous CAD engineer who works for Four Leaves Technology, whose real name, appearance, and profile are all shrouded in mystery! The genius programmer, the first in the world to implement the Loop Cast System!

"Oh, the Loop Cast System is, well. Normally, your activation program is erased every time you activate magic, and in order to execute the same technique again, the activation program needs to be reexpanded from the CAD, but loop casting is an activation program where you add the ability to take the activation program during the final phase and make a copy of it in your magic calculation region, which lets the magician keep activating the same magic for as far as their calculative capacities can handle it, which was all supposed to be possible in theory for a long time, but they could never quite distribute the calculative ability well enough to handle both the execution of the magic and the duplication of the activation program, so—"

"Okay, okay! We know what loop casting is."

"Is that so…? Anyway, the Silver Horn is the name of a specialized CAD model that was fully customized by Taurus Silver! Obviously it's optimized for loop casting, and even its ability to activate magic smoothly with the minimum amount of magic power received high reviews, and in particular, it's superpopular among the police! So much so that despite being a model currently in production, it's been featured in tons of premium deals! And that one is a limited-edition model where the gun barrel is longer than a normal Silver Horn, isn't it? Where on earth did you get that?"

"Ah-chan, calm down a little, okay?"

Her chest was rising and falling heavily—had she run out of breath?—and her eyes were heart-shaped as she gazed at Tatsuya's hands. If Mayumi hadn't chided her, she might have gotten so close that she would have pressed her face against it.

On the other hand, Mayumi's head tilted again with a new question. "But, Rin, that's still strange, isn't it? His CAD may be highly efficient and optimized for loop casting, but loop casting in the first place, it's..."

Suzune tilted her own head as well when this subject was broached instead of nodding. "Yes, it is odd. Loop casting is purely used to activate the same exact magic more than once. He may have used vibration magic all three times, but loop casting automatically keeps creating whatever the magician sets up. It couldn't have created multiple waves with the differing frequencies needed for that constructive interference. You can probably create different frequency waves in sequence required for the interference with the same activation program if you made the part that determines the frequency into a variable, but if you had to make that into a variable *along with* the coordinates, intensity, and duration... Are you telling me you pulled all that off?"

This time, Suzune had stumbled on her words for real. Tatsuya casually shrugged off her gaze. "Multiple variables aren't part of evaluating processing speed, or calculation scope, or interference intensity, after all." Mayumi and Mari stared at him fixedly, and Tatsuya answered them by bragging with the same uninterested tone of voice as before.

"...One's evaluation of magical power during the practical exam is decided by the speed at which he activates the magic, the scope of the magic program, and the intensity with which he overwrites the target information. I see—I guess this is another example of tests not measuring someone's true abilities..."

The groaned answer to Tatsuya's cynical words came from Hattori, who had sat up on the floor.

"Hanzou, are you all right?" Mayumi bent over a bit and leaned forward and looked at him.

"I'm okay!" Hattori hastily stood up, as if to get away from her suddenly close face.

"I'm sure. You were awake the whole time, after all." Hattori's words couldn't have been spoken if he hadn't heard what the girls had been talking about. Mayumi straightened back up and nodded, convinced.

Hattori replied to her, "No, I actually wasn't conscious at first!" His face went red, and he urgently began explaining himself again. "Even after I woke back up, everything was hazy... I only got control of my body back just now!"

He looked very—how to put it?—Tatsuya could easily predict what kind of emotion he was feeling.

"Is that so...? Nevertheless, you seem to have understood everything we've been talking about."

"... I mean, even though it was hazy, it still got to my ears, I guess..."

And it seemed Mayumi herself was fully aware of the emotions Hattori directed at her.

Is she evil?

But there was something out of place between the image evoked by the word *evil* and the atmosphere she gave off, so Tatsuya stopped thinking about it. He had also realized it didn't really matter all that much. He got back to what he'd been doing before Mari stopped him.

...Though it was nothing that exaggerated—he was just putting his CAD back in the case. He pretended not to notice Azusa's wishful staring at his hands. And he ignored his sister's gaze as she tried to help him.

Because Miyuki wasn't very good with machines.

She wasn't completely averse to technology or anything, but because his CAD was tuned very specifically, it wasn't something a normal high school student would be able to deal with. (On the other hand, CADs given only the most minor of adjustments, like the practical ones used in school, wouldn't let Tatsuya fully display his skill.) Even if Miyuki helped, the truth was she would only end up making it take longer.

As Tatsuya was rummaging around, resetting the security and exchanging the cartridge, he heard footsteps and felt a presence approach him from behind. It looked like his excuses were over. He didn't mind leaving what he was doing until later, but he still didn't turn around.

"Shiba…"

"Yes?" answered Miyuki in an evasive tenor.

There were only two males in this room, and one was Tatsuya. Even if his tone of voice made him sound like a different person, there was no mistaking who was talking.

"About before, well… I said some rude things, like you having favoritism."

And there was no doubt about who the voice was speaking to, either.

"No, my eyes were what were clouded. I hope you can forgive me."

"No, I said some pretty cheeky things. Please forgive me."

He knew even over his back that he was bowing very deeply.

Tatsuya locked his case shut, smirking at Miyuki's adult behavior. Just who was the older sibling here, anyway?

Then, he deliberately turned around.

Hattori's face betrayed a momentary falter, but he immediately regained his self-assured expression.

Was this breather in preparation of making a truce or a herald of a rematch?

Those possibilities both disappeared without being realized. In the end, Hattori and Tatsuya simply glared at each other, and the former turned on his heel.

He sensed that Miyuki beside him was a little miffed, so he gently patted her shoulder.

She would be working with Hattori in the student council from today on, so it wouldn't do her any good to let this leave a bad taste in her mouth. As if Miyuki understood his intent, she quickly calmed down.

"Let's go back to the student council room," suggested Mayumi. With that, everyone present began to move.

As Suzune, Azusa, and Hattori followed behind her, Mayumi looked like she wanted to complain about something.

Mari was behind them. When she realized Tatsuya was looking at her, she shrugged to him without letting the other four see.

◇ ◇ ◇

After Tatsuya gave his CAD back to the office, he came back to the student council room. As soon as he got there, Mari suddenly latched on to his arm.

Miyuki, being taught how to use the workstation along the wall by Azusa, looked to him and raised her eyebrows. He tried to send her a *I couldn't do anything about it* message with his eyes…but he doubted whether she understood it. He might have had a momentary lapse as he forced his body *not* to give its automatic reaction of throwing Mari off of him, but the girl still seemed to have quite a high level of martial ability.

"Okay, a whole bunch of unplanned things happened, but let's get to the committee room. That was the original plan, after all."

Without regard for Tatsuya's inner thoughts (which were mostly ones of bewilderment), Mari pulled his arm along.

After seeing Tatsuya make an uncooperative face, Miyuki finally returned her eyes to the terminal—albeit reluctantly.

Hattori hadn't looked up from what he was doing even once since Tatsuya entered the room. It seemed like he had come to terms with his emotions and had decided on ignoring him. That was something Tatsuya was grateful for as well.

Mayumi was thoughtlessly waving to him with only her hand.

What did she want to do—or say...? She was probably the most baffling person he had met here.

But that, too, was something for later. He struggled (well, *pretended* to struggle) to get his arm out of Mari's, then obediently followed her.

There was a direct staircase down to the disciplinary committee headquarters in the back of the room, where there would normally be an emergency escape.

Are they ignoring fire safety regulations? thought Tatsuya, but despite the students being just that—in training, magicians in the making—there still wasn't much point in adhering to fire laws in a place filled with superior magicians. One could get rid of fire by using vibration and deceleration magic, and smoke could be eliminated with binding/movement compound magic. In reality, large-scale fires in superskyscrapers were one of the most spectacular arenas for magicians.

He changed his mind—he supposed he could let it slide as long as it wasn't an elevator.

He followed her through the back door and set foot into the headquarters. Mari indicated the chairs in front of a long table.

"It's a bit of a mess, but you can sit wherever you like."

A *bit*?

Certainly, it wasn't so messy that you couldn't move across the floor or couldn't sit down because of things piled up on the chairs.

But having just come from the extremely neat and tidy student council room, he couldn't help but feel a bit of resistance to calling this "a bit messy."

Documents, books, portable terminals, CADs—things of all kinds were burying the surface of the long desk table. There was a chair pulled halfway out, so he strolled over that way and took a seat.

"The disciplinary committee is like an all-male household. I keep telling them pretty strictly to keep everything in order here, but..."

"If nobody's here, then it's not going to get clean." Tatsuya's remark could be taken as sarcasm or comfort—Mari's eyebrow twitched.

"…Well, patrolling school grounds is our main job. We can't help the room being empty."

The two of them were currently the only ones in there. The disciplinary committee had nine members, but this deserted room seemed like it could fit twice that. It made the mess amplify the sense of chaos in the room. Of course, Tatsuya wasn't paying attention to the state of affairs of the room as a whole, but the various items all over the table.

"Either way, Chairwoman, can I clean these things up?"

"What…?" Tatsuya's sudden request caused Mari to raise an eyebrow in surprise.

—Contrary to his expectations, she seemed to be the dramatic type.

"As someone striving to be a magic engineer, it's difficult for me to endure seeing CADs in such a disorderly state. And it looks like there are terminals here that have been left in hibernation." Still, though, it didn't change Tatsuya's response.

"A magic engineer? Even though you have personal combat skills like that?" Mari seriously seemed confused by what he said.

The duel before ended pretty simply and easily, but high-level personal combat skills that could be described as "insane" had been used during it.

"With my talents, I wouldn't be able to get any more than a Class C license, no matter how much I struggled."

However, when Mari tried to argue against his masochistic answer, which he gave like it was none of his concern, she was astonished to find that she couldn't find the words to do it with.

In many countries, magicians were managed with a license system. Many of those places had introduced a national standard of license issuing, and this country was one of them. Whether for employment at a corporation, in a public office, or for starting your own business, a certain license was required to do jobs depending on their difficulty. It was set up so that those with higher-ranked licenses would be paid higher rewards. There were five levels in the international licensing system, from A to E. Being chosen for a license was based on one's speed, scale, and level of interference of constructing and executing magic programs, just like the practical skills evaluation in schools. In fact, the schools' skills evaluation standards were created to be in alignment with the international license evaluation standards.

There were some places using special standards such as the police force and the military, but in those cases you would be evaluated only as an officer or as a soldier, not as a magician.

"...Anyway, may I clean the table up?"

"Hm? Oh, yeah. I'll help too. I can give you the rundown as we work." She hastily rose. Maybe she was a more considerate person than she seemed.

Though maybe Tatsuya, who had begun organizing the documents in front of him, was more impudent for still sitting down.

Of course, the fact that feelings and results didn't necessarily match up was just how the world worked. The speed at which they worked was the same, but for some reason, in contrast to Tatsuya steadily creating a space around his hands, he still couldn't see a glimpse of the surface of the long desk in front of Mari.

Tatsuya glanced up at her.

Then he sighed a little.

Mari gave up and stopped. "Sorry. No matter how hard I try, I'm just bad at this."

Tatsuya thought to himself that maybe the current state of the room was mostly her responsibility. He was adult enough not to say what he thought, however.

"You really seem to know what you're doing, though."

"With what?"

"Filing papers. I thought you were just piling them up at random, but they're all properly sorted and everything."

"...Sorry, could you not do that...?"

Perhaps now becoming serious, Mari was glancing at him flipping through the piles of papers, about to lean herself on the desk and sit in the space he had cleared. It made her skirt hem nearly touch his arm. Her long and slender lower legs and calves were stretching from her skirt, which subtly hid her thighs. He may not have been able to see her skin through her leggings, but he could still see how they were shaped—and that was enough to be undesirable for his mental health.

"Oh, sorry."

She didn't sound sorry at all, but this, too, was something he didn't need to point out. —If she had been doing it on purpose, it had obviously had the opposite effect, and as they say, silence is golden.

Tatsuya silently moved his chair and got to work on the next area. He dug out a few book stands from the piles of papers and began to stand books on them. Both paper books and book stands were rare items in this day and age. Even more so if they happened to be grimoires.

"The reason I scouted you—come to think of it, I explained most of it already, huh? Making punishments for attempted criminals more appropriate, and to repair our image toward Course 2 students."

"I remember, but for the image part, wouldn't that have the opposite effect?" Finished with straightening up the books, he got to work on the terminals. "...Can I look at these?"

His request for permission to look at the work-in-progress data on them was granted by an affirmative nod. He turned the hibernating terminals back on, then shut them down, left them in their closed states, and gathered them all into one place.

"Why do you think so?"

"We could never interfere in anything before now. If you were suddenly under the control of another underclassman who you thought was in the same situation, you wouldn't think it was very funny."

He rose from his seat and started rummaging through a cabinet on the wall. As he piled the terminals on the empty shelf, he heard the irresponsible reply of "I guess that's true."

"I think the other Course 1 students would welcome it, though. You've at least talked about it to your classmates, right?"

"Well, I have, but…" After he finished lining up the terminals, he fished around in another cabinet. "I think it would cause twice as much animosity for them as it would welcoming."

He found what he was looking for. He stood up straight and turned his shoulders, taking off his jacket and rolling up his shirtsleeves.

"Well, they're gonna feel animosity. But they just enrolled a couple days ago. I don't think they've been that poisoned by discriminatory thoughts yet."

"I wonder about that." Tatsuya rummaged through the items inside the cabinet, then his hands came back out holding a CAD case. "I've already gotten one of those *I won't accept you* declarations yesterday, after all."

He wrapped his exposed wrist in a grounding wristband and reached out for the big clump of CADs.

"You carry something like that around? …Are you talking about Morisaki?"

"It's actually pretty handy… Do you know about him?"

"He's gonna be part of the committee—he's the teachers' recommendation."

"Wha—?"

The strength drained from his hands checking the CADs' status. He hastily grabbed it back up before it fell back down on the desk.

"Huh, I guess even you get surprised."

"Well, yes!" Mari began to grin, and Tatsuya answered her with a sigh. He wished she'd stop with this weird sense of rivalry.

"He caused an issue yesterday, so I can get them to repeal their recommendation. I actually planned to do that, but you're not unrelated to the incident, either."

"I *am* a concerned party."

"Yeah. I scouted someone who claims to have been involved, so it would be hard to refuse *him*."

"Why not just not let either of us in?"

"Do you not want to?"

Tatsuya stopped working again at the sudden, straightforward question.

For now, he placed the CAD in his hands inside the case, then looked up. Mari was sitting up against the desk, looking down at him. She wasn't smiling. She was giving him a piercing, eyes-half-closed stare.

"...In all honesty, I think it'll be a pain."

"Hmph... And?"

"It'll be a pain, but I also don't think I can withdraw at this point."

A mean-spirited, complacent smile rose to Mari's face again. Its crookedness brought her sharp beauty 20 percent higher.

"You have things tough, too, don't you...?"

"And you're pretty twisted, too."

Unfortunately, Tatsuya had to admit that she had him there.

◇ ◇ ◇

"...This *is* the disciplinary committee headquarters, right?"

That was the first thing out of Mayumi's mouth when she came down the stairs.

"How's that for a greeting?"

"I mean, what happened, Mari? No matter how much Rin warns you, no matter how much Ah-chan pleads with you, you've never tried to clean up before!"

"I will firmly oppose such baseless slander, Mayumi! It wasn't that I never tried to; it's that I never actually cleaned it!"

"For a girl, that seems even more troubling." Mayumi gave her a narrow-eyed, slanted glare, and Mari immediately turned her face away.

"It doesn't really matter... But yes, that's how it is."

After setting eyes on Tatsuya, who was peering into the maintenance hatch of a fixed terminal, Mayumi nodded, convinced.

"So he's making himself useful right away, then."

"Well, that should do it," he answered with his back still to them. He shut the hatch and turned around. "Chairwoman, my inspection is finished. I swapped out a few damaged-looking parts, so you shouldn't have any further issues."

"Thanks a lot." Mari nodded, relaxed, but it somehow looked like there was a bit of sweat forming around her temple.

A cold sweat.

"I see… Since he called you Chairwoman, you must have successfully recruited him," said Mayumi in a carefree voice, bursting with understanding and acceptance. She put on her own malicious smile.

Tatsuya answered without looking at her. "I don't really think I had any right to refuse in the first place…"

Mayumi didn't seem to appreciate the attitude. She put one hand on her hip, then stuck her other index finger out at him, puffed out a cheek, and glared at him with sulking eyes. As far as he could tell, the whole thing was a huge act. She argued, "Tatsuya, I'm like your big sister here. Don't you think you should treat me a little more nicely?"

…Tatsuya immediately wanted to tell her that he *had* no big sister. He got the feeling saying so would only make his situation worse, so he refrained. She was so stereotypical in everything she did that it wasn't creative at all.

Tatsuya secretly thought to himself that *she* should be the one treating *him* a little more respectfully.

He had gotten this impression drifting through the air this whole time…but now, for some reason, it was something he didn't feel like ignoring.

"President, this is just to make sure, but there's something I want to know."

"Hm? What is it?"

"We never met each other before the day of the entrance ceremony, right?" Tatsuya asked, filled with an intent of *Aren't you acting overfamiliar with me?* Mayumi's eyes widened.

However, they rapidly returned to their former size, and as

they narrowed further, her smile, which could only be described as "wicked," covered her alluring face.

Tatsuya realized he had just made an extremely poor decision.

He remembered when Mari made the same sort of smile. *I see— birds of a feather really do flock together*, he thought, trying to escape reality.

"I see, I see how it is... Heh-heh-heh-heh..."

The word *impish* described her smile to a tee.

"Tatsuya, you think you actually met me before that, do you? That our meeting on the day of the entrance ceremony was fate!"

"No, umm, President?"

What on earth was she so excited about?

"Maybe we met each other far in the past. Two people, pulled apart by fate, once again brought together by it!"

If she really was enraptured by this idea, it would just make her a very dangerous person. But the part where she was making sure he could tell she was putting on a conscious act made her even worse.

"...Unfortunately, though, that was definitely our first meeting."

"...I thought as much."

"Mm! Did you feel like it was destiny? Did you?"

She made fists in front of her chest and started moving toward him, looking up at his face. ——She was excited. Oh, how sly she was. And it suited her so well... She was truly wicked.

"...I'm sorry. Why are you having so much fun?" He answered her question with another, but still didn't receive an answer.

She only continued to look at him, filled with hopefulness. *She's a sadist*, noted Tatsuya to himself.

Anyway, he probably needed to answer her. Tatsuya sighed, almost as if breathing out smoke, and answered after a moment. "...If this is fate, then it's not destiny—it's doom, for sure."

His answer made Mayumi's face cloud over and she turned away. A lonely murmur of "Oh..." reached Tatsuya's ears. Her form, seen from behind, radiated sorrow.

Tatsuya was aware he had said something pretty brutal. He had said it because he'd judged Mayumi to be entirely fooling around. But if even a little bit of how she was acting was real, he decided he needed to apologize.

However. His sense of guilt didn't last very long—whether fortunately or unfortunately. In this case, him not knowing immediately what to do had borne fruit.

"…Damn."

Something leaked from her mouth as if she had been outlasted, her shoulders drooping in dejection.

This time it was Tatsuya's turn to widen his eyes. It was very faint, but it was certainly not a classy thing to say—did she just *swear*?

"Umm, President?"

"Yes, what is it?" When she turned back around, her face had the classy smile that had charmed all of the new male students.

"…I feel like I'm beginning to understand you better."

In front of the exhausted Tatsuya, Mayumi had removed her false mask and showed him her true face.

In other words, her wicked smile.

"Let's stop with the jokes, shall we? Tatsuya doesn't seem to take well to it." Mayumi, without a modicum of guilt, declared everything had been a joke.

"It's not gonna go like how it did with Hattori, Mayumi. Doesn't seem like your charms work on him," said Mari teasingly, just when it counted.

Mayumi couldn't let that one pass. She made a testy face and responded, "Please, don't say anything so scandalous. It makes me sound like I'm toying with any underclassman I can get my hands on."

Regretting having asked a careless question, Tatsuya began trying to put things back together. If these two poisoned him any further, it would be his own faults on display this time. "Umm, well. What I wanted to ask was—"

"Mayumi having a different attitude toward you is a sign she approves of you, Tatsuya. She probably felt that the two of you have something in common. This girl feigns innocence all the time. She can't show her true colors except to people she approves of." Mari's expression suddenly became serious, and Tatsuya felt a sense of imbalance in it.

"Don't trust anything Mari says, Tatsuya! But I guess it's true that I approve of you. You don't really feel like a stranger. Maybe I'm actually the one who felt like it was destiny."

You couldn't hate that face, so mischievous she might have stuck out her tongue. It threw off his pace even more.

Seems I don't have much of a chance of winning against these two head-on, he thought.

◇ ◇ ◇

Mayumi had come downstairs to tell them that she'd be closing up the student council room for the day. And she had used the opportunity to see how Tatsuya was doing, but that ending up being the main purpose of her coming down here probably wasn't his imagination.

They had been busy with all sorts of things right after the entrance ceremony, and they'd reached a place where they could pause.

"Okay, then I'll see you up there!" Mayumi waved her hand and went back up to the student council room.

Starting tomorrow, things would get noisy because of the contest every club would participate in once to recruit new club members. Since the disciplinary committee would start having more to do because of it, even Tatsuya and Mari had just been talking about calling it quits for the day.

Modern information systems didn't require the time to start up and shut down like they used to. You just switched it off—and then you could leave it lying on the floor for months without anything happening to it. Even if you forgot to hit the switch, it would automatically go into hibernation. He had already completely and thoroughly organized them, so now all he had to do was set up their security features.

But just then, with perfect timing—or maybe bad timing—two male students entered the disciplinary committee headquarters.

"G'morning!"

"Good morning!"

The brisk, assertive voices rang throughout the room.

"Whoa, big sis, you were here?"

Where am I and what time period is this? thought Tatsuya.

The short-haired guy, who wasn't very tall but had an awfully rugged build—the sort a headband would make sense on—had called someone *Ane-san* as though they were very accustomed to doing so.

They must be talking about Watanabe... He looked at the person in question, and she looked subtly embarrassed. He felt an out-of-place relief at the fact that she had normal sensitivities, slight though they may have been.

"Chairwoman, we have completed our patrols for the day! No arrests were made!"

The other one had a relatively normal appearance and a relatively normal way of speaking, but his posture was excessively proper.

His report, delivered while standing at attention, gave him the air of a soldier, or police officer, or perhaps a kid who hadn't grown out of his energetic phase.

"...Could you have cleaned up the room, big sis?"

The first guy looked around the completely changed state of the room in suspicion and began to walk toward the dumbfounded Tatsuya. He didn't look that heavy, but strangely, the term *lumbering* would have fit his gait.

As soon as he saw Mari nonchalantly stand in his way—

"Ow!"

Whap!

There was a satisfying noise, and the guy was crouching on the floor holding his head.

In Mari's hand was a firmly rolled-up notebook that she had taken out at some point.

Where on earth had she gotten it from?

"Don't call me 'big sis'! How many times must I tell you before you understand?! Is your head just a decoration, Koutarou?!" shouted Mari angrily at the male student, now cradling his head, completely ignorant of Tatsuya's questions.

"Please, stop hitting me like that, Bi—er, Chairwoman. By the way, who is he? A new recruit?" grumbled the male student named Koutarou without seeming like he was in very much pain. He hastily changed the title he was using when she jabbed the notebook in his face with lightning speed.

Mari's shoulders drooped before the face of Koutarou stiffened in nervousness, and she sighed. "Yes, he's a new recruit. Tatsuya Shiba, from 1-E. He's here as the student council's nominee."

"Huh… You're a crestless?" Koutarou looked in fascination at Tatsuya's blazer and then took a good look at his figure.

"Tatsumi, that expression borders on prohibited terms! I think you should call him a Course 2 student in this case!" Though Koutarou seemed to be appraising Tatsuya, the other male student didn't try to caution his attitude itself.

"You know, he'll pull the rug out from under you if you underestimate him. This is just between us, but Hattori just came back from getting the rug pulled out from under *him*." But Mari told them the truth with a grin, like she was teasing them, and their expression immediately grew more serious.

"…Do you mean this guy beat *Hattori*?"

"Yeah. In an official duel."

"Amazing! Hattori, undefeated since enrolling here, lost to a new student?"

"Don't shout like that, Sawaki. I told you to this is just between us, remember?"

It was extremely discomforting to be looked at so intently, but they seemed to be upperclassmen and his seniors in the disciplinary committee. His only option here was to endure it.

"That's pretty reassuring!"

"So he's got talent, Chairwoman?"

Their expressions changed so simply it was almost anticlimactic. The speed at which they switched—he wanted to call it admirable.

"Weren't expecting that, huh?"

"Huh?"

It was all so sudden, and he didn't understand what he'd been asked. Luckily, Mari didn't seem to be expecting an answer when she asked it.

"This school is filled with people basking in superiority and drowning in inferiority because of the stupid titles Bloom and Weed. Honestly, I'm just sick of it. So the match today was a rather thrilling experience, I have to say. Fortunately, Mayumi and Juumonji both know I'm like this. The student council and club association only choose people that have relatively less of that sense. They can't get anyone who has *zero* sense of superiority, but they're all people with great actual skill. Unfortunately, it didn't go all the way to the third person—elected by the teachers—but for you, this should be a pretty comfortable place."

"I'm Koutarou Tatsumi from 3-C. Nice to be workin' with you, Shiba. We'll welcome anyone skilled with open arms."

"I'm Midori Sawaki from 2-D. Welcome to the club, Shiba!"

Koutarou and Sawaki both wanted a handshake.

As Mari said, there was no hint of disdain or contempt on their faces.

He now knew that they had been appraising him on his real ability from the very beginning and didn't care a bit whether he was a Course 1 or Course 2 student.

It was, indeed, a little unexpected. And it certainly wasn't a bad atmosphere, either.

He returned their greetings, then took Sawaki's hand. But for some reason, Sawaki didn't let go.

"Juumonji is the president of the extracurricular activities oversight committee, or the club committee for short."

Was it so he could tell him that? But he could have let go of his hand if that was all it was.

"Also, call me by my last name—Sawaki."

The force he was putting into his hand snapped Tatsuya back to reality. He was squeezing so hard it might have creaked like a floorboard, and Tatsuya couldn't suppress his surprise.

It seemed like students excelling in more than just magic had gathered at this school.

"Please, take care not to call me by my first name."

That seemed to be a warning.

He didn't have to be so roundabout with him—Tatsuya wasn't in the habit of calling his upperclassmen by their first names, but he had to *politely return* his *greeting.*

"I'll keep that in mind," he answered, twisting his right hand slightly and pulling it from Sawaki's.

Tatsuya's display of martial prowess brought surprise more to Koutarou's face than Sawaki's himself. "Hey, you're pretty good, aren't you? Sawaki's grip is almost a hundred kilos."

"...Yes, certainly not the strength of a magician," he replied lightly, putting himself aside.

At the very least, he felt like he'd be able to get along with these two.

[4]

CADs were the symbol of the superiority of modern magic, having made faster, more delicate, more complex, more wide-scale magic possible, compared to the traditional support tools like wands, grimoires, and amulets.

But they were not actually superior to traditional tools in *every* way.

They were precise instruments and required more frequent maintenance than traditional tools. Tuning the transmission and reception systems that were aligned with the psionic wave properties of the user was especially important.

CADs used the psions sent from the magician as the main ingredient (or perhaps ink, or paint, would be a more suitable analogy) to output activation programs, which were psionic information bodies. Skin was a good conductor of psions, so the magician would absorb the activation programs through it and use it as a blueprint to build a magic program. It was said that spells using a CAD could vary from 5 to 10 percent in activation speed depending on how well tuned the CAD was.

Psions were said to be particles embodying thoughts and intentions. Everyone had their own sort of thoughts. If you had a hundred people, there would be a hundred kinds—if a thousand people, then a thousand kinds. Psionic waves had traits that differed slightly from person to person, and CADs that hadn't been tuned to that wouldn't be able to conduct the exchange of psions with the magician as well.

There were plenty of other aspects that made the CAD easier to use, too.

Tuning CADs was the job of magic engineers, and this was the reason skilled ones were so highly prized.

Incidentally, the properties of psionic waves would change with the growth or decay of one's body, and they could even be influenced by one's current physical condition. Strictly speaking, it changed on a day-to-day basis.

So by nature, it was desirable to perform adjustments according to the user's physical state every day, but adjusting CADs required fairly expensive and dedicated equipment.

If you were the army, the police, a central government agency, a top-class research institution, a famous school, or a large corporation with vast assets, you could get the CAD-adjusting equipment and personnel by yourself, but at the mid- to small-business or personal level, you couldn't really set up a place to tune them in your own home. For magicians belonging to such places, bringing their CAD for routine inspection to a magic device specialty shop or the manufacturer's service station once or twice a month was as much as they could do.

First High was a top-class, elite school even in this country, so as one might expect, it featured school-use adjustment facilities. Normally, students would bring teachers and tune their CADs at school.

But due to special circumstances, there was brand-new CAD adjustment equipment set up right in Tatsuya's house.

◇ ◇ ◇

After dinner, Tatsuya had gone down to the basement, which had been remodeled into a workroom, to tune his own CADs, when he heard the voice of essentially the only other person living here.

"Don't be shy. Come in. I was just reaching a good spot to take a break."

He wasn't lying. In fact, Miyuki had spoken to him precisely because she had estimated when he would be reaching that break point.

"Excuse me. Tatsuya, could you adjust my CAD for me…?"

In her hands was her portable terminal-shaped CAD.

As she approached, more of the pleasant, faint smell of soap tickled his nasal cavities.

She was wearing a simple gown, like the kind a patient at a hospital might wear for an examination.

"Are your settings not right?"

It was the standard wear when having adjustments done.

"Oh, heavens no! Your adjustments are always perfect."

Her excessive praise was par for the course, so he didn't bother trying to correct her. He had enough experience to realize that arguing over it would be too unproductive.

But he had just done a full maintenance on it three days ago. Normally he did that once a week, so she must have had some sudden reason for it.

"It's just that, well…"

"You don't need to hesitate. I always tell you that, right?"

"I'm sorry. Actually, I was wondering if you could swap my activation programs…"

"What, was that all? You really didn't need to beat around the bush. It just makes me worried instead."

He mussed up his sister's hair a little and took the CAD from her hands.

Miyuki looked down, a little embarrassed.

"What family do you want to add?"

Ninety-nine activation programs could be recorded in a multipurpose CAD at one time. This was a limit that didn't change, even for Miyuki's CAD, which had been further tuned even from the latest technology.

On the other hand, variations on those activation programs were practically infinite based on how much of the program you wanted to be hard-coded and how much you wanted your own magic calculation region to deal with.

In general, people adopted a pattern where the coordinates, intensity, and ending conditions were given as variables as additional processing for their magic calculation region, while other factors were built into the activation program. However, plenty of people would instead build the intensity into the activation program so they could decrease the calculations needed and increase the casting speed. There were many defensive magic programs that used one's own relative coordinates as a fixed value, too, and practice classes would introduce techniques using contact magic that made all values fixed.

In contrast to those examples, Miyuki liked to register activation programs that were more flexible by eliminating as many of those fixed values as possible.

Miyuki could master far more numerous and more varied types of magic than the average magician was able to learn, and she was only fifteen. For her, the ninety-nine-spell limit was too small.

"Binding-type activation programs... I want to increase the number of personal combat variations."

"Hm? I wouldn't think, with your deceleration magic, that you'd need to have more in the way of binding magic."

Even among her extensively diverse trump cards, she particularly specialized in deceleration magic. With cooling magic, a variation of the deceleration type, she was even able to approximate a state of absolute zero.

"As you are well aware, most of deceleration magic consists of techniques that apply to an entire person, and it's hard to apply them to single parts. Slowing down or cooling individual parts isn't impossible, but it takes too much time to cast. I had a thought while observing today's duel. I believe I am lacking in spells placing an emphasis on speed that can disable an opponent while doing the least amount of damage."

"Hmm... I don't really think you're the type for that, though. Surprising opponents and confusing them with your speed is a tactic, but your magic power is absolute and overwhelming. Isn't a more orthodox strategy a better fit—nullifying an opponent's magic by interfering with the area around them, then hitting them with magic that outclasses the scope and strength of their defensive capabilities?"

Area interference was a technique to nullify an opponent's magic by placing the space around yourself under the effects of your magic power. By covering a fixed region with magic that said "events here cannot be altered," you could obstruct the opponent's magic-induced event alteration.

As Tatsuya said, Miyuki's area interference was incredibly powerful. Even if she lost the initiative in a magic fight, there was almost no chance of her sustaining damage. The basic tactic in magical combat of being the first one to land an attack on the opponent wasn't actually a very high priority for Miyuki.

"...Will you not do it?"

But Tatsuya didn't say no to his timidly questioning sister.

"No, there's nothing I won't do. Let's see... In the student council, in terms of strategy against student opponents from the same school, you might need this sort of thing. All right. I'll try adjusting your activation programs in the same family so that I don't have to shave off some of the magic you have now."

When coaxed by Miyuki, Tatsuya would never refuse. But he didn't forget to give her some advice.

"You should really think about carrying another CAD with you."

"You're the only one who can use two CADs at once, Tatsuya."

"I'm telling you, you could do it, too, if you tried."

Miyuki turned away in a huff, and he stroked her hair a few times while grinning drily. Rubbing her hair or her head was Tatsuya's basic solution for getting his sister's mood to improve.

The effects were immediate.

Miyuki narrowed her eyes in pleasure at the gentle feeling of her brother's hand snugly on her small head.

"Then let's take your measurements first," he said with a technician's face, once he saw that his sister's mood had improved.

Miyuki took a step back, reluctant to pull herself away from the sensation of his palm, and smoothly took off her gown.

What appeared was her immodest, half-naked self.

The only thing covering her body as she lay down on the measurement table was her white underwear.

The pure, snow-white color—the situation was changed to an extraordinarily lascivious color.

Even if she was his sister—no, *because* Miyuki was an incomparable beauty, he shouldn't have been able to remain calm in this situation. Her body's abundant charms would drive any man crazy.

But when Tatsuya's eyes met her gaze teeming with unhidden embarrassment, they didn't show a single hint of emotion.

He had become a living, breathing machine, constructed to observe, analyze, and record.

Without entertaining any emotion, and acknowledging the situation for what it was, Tatsuya had become the realization of the ideal state that magicians hoped to reach.

◇ ◇ ◇

"All right, you're all done."

At Tatsuya's signal, Miyuki sat up on the table.

This sort of measurement wasn't something that was performed just anywhere.

In fact, adjustments involving such precise measurements were on the rarer side.

At the school's facilities, you would put on a headset and place your hands on a panel to get it to measure you.

Tatsuya handed Miyuki her gown back without looking at her. As she put it on, she glared at Tatsuya's back with a glum face.

Her brother was sitting on his backless chair, facing his terminal as if nothing had happened.

No, there was no "as if."

Nothing had actually happened, and he did this every week.

If he let himself pay attention to this, there would be no end to his worries.

It wouldn't make his embarrassment go away, and he also didn't want to get rid of it entirely—but above that, he didn't think anything.

He was making a point not to think about anything else.

Her brother remaining calm was something Miyuki was grateful for as well.

——Usually, anyway.

"You're mean, Tatsuya..."

"Miyuki?"

Tatsuya's voice was overturned by Miyuki's coquettish whisper.

——Her brother's agitated, confused voice, which she heard only very rarely.

——He found himself with that voice, a discomposed heartbeat, a heightening body temperature, and a mysterious satisfaction.

Miyuki, with her gown on but not closed in the front, nestled into his back as if to get him to carry her. As she rubbed her cheek to his, as she pressed her soft, twin bulges against his back, she continued to whisper into her brother's ear.

"Your sister is so embarrassed, and yet you always look so calm..."

"Um, Miyuki, what?"

"Or do you not include me as part of the opposite gender?"

"It would be bad if I did!"

It was a sound argument. However, the moment it manifested into words, they became chains of iron, dragging that which he didn't need to think about to the forefront of his mind.

"Am I not to your liking? Do you prefer people like Saegusa? Or do you prefer people like Mari? You were talking to them quite intimately today..."

"You were listening?"

She couldn't have been.

Miyuki had been learning how to use the information systems in the student council room from Azusa the whole time.

Besides, if she *had* tried to eavesdrop, there would have been no way he wouldn't have noticed it.

But he didn't have the kind of time to build and systematize an argument against her.

"Well, I knew it! I suppose they are beautiful, aren't they?"

"Hello? Miyuki? Are you misunderstanding something here?"

"Ogling all the beautiful upperclassmen surrounding you…"

At some point Miyuki's hand had grabbed her CAD.

"…Tatsuya needs to be punished!"

"Gwah!"

Caught completely by surprise and at his wit's end, Tatsuya's body convulsed from the vibration wave fired by Miyuki, and he slid out of his chair and to the floor.

Self-repair technique starting automatically. Reloading core eidos data from backup. Loading magic programs…complete. Self-repair… complete.

The span of time he'd been unconscious was less than one second.

He didn't release his consciousness for more than a moment.

He wouldn't allow himself to go down for more than a moment.

That was *his original* magic—and it was like a curse.

When he naturally opened his eyes, there was a flowery countenance looking at him from above.

"Good morning, Tatsuya."

"…Have I done something to make you mad?"

"I really apologize. My practical joke went too far."

Though her lips apologized, her face smiled. It was a cute smile, appropriate for her age. His sister rarely relaxed her mature attitude outside the house.

The only thought that came to mind when confronted with such a smile was that, well, it didn't really matter anyway.

It really was a pair of siblings messing around childishly.

Whatever extreme measures she took, she was incapable of hurting him with finality.

"Give me a break…"

He grabbed her outstretched hand and, while his mouth was grumbling, his face, too, was smiling.

◇ ◇ ◇

She awoke at the usual time.

But she felt like she had a harder time this morning than usual.

She was a little dazed.

She couldn't sense her brother in the house.

He had probably left for his morning training.

This was usual, too.

Her brother stayed up later than her every night and woke up earlier than her every morning.

Waking up earlier than him like she had the day before yesterday really was a rare occurrence.

She had worried about him hurting himself in the past.

Now she knew that was needless anxiety.

Her brother, that person—he was special.

People around him called her a genius.

They praised her as special, somebody different from them.

——*They don't know anything.*

The really amazing one, the really special one, the true genius, is my brother.

He is in a different dimension.

They don't understand.

Those girls giving me compliments while hiding their envy will never understand.

Truly isolated talent goes beyond jealousy—it inspires fear.
Not awe, but fear.

She knew. She knew how their father, overcome with that fear, had treated his flesh and blood, and how unfair his behavior was.

Her brother believed that she didn't know about it.

So she pretended she didn't.

Their father—that man despised her brother's talents. He had given him a false sense of failure. Even now, he was plotting how he would break her brother's mind, his spirit, and those wings of his that could carry him far above the skies. She actually knew about that.

It was absurd.

He had tried to chain him up and throw him in the corner, but in the end, he was made fully aware of how much his son's talents surpassed his own.

He eventually gave him assets to compensate for his freedom.

He watched as his powers of restraining, his one and only talent, crumbled before his very eyes.

The only thing that man had done was force upon him a false name and steal from him the admiration of the world.

Even though the man must have known her brother had no interest in such things.

…She was losing control of her thoughts.

She began to feel like she was someone else.

She got the feeling she wasn't entirely awake yet.

Maybe she hadn't gotten enough sleep.

She knew the reason.

It was because of what happened last night.

She had been calm at the time.

Her confused brother had seemed funny for once—even cute.

Her emotions had surpassed his.

But she left him, then went alone to her room and lay down in bed—and then she couldn't remain calm.

The throbbing in her chest wouldn't let her sleep.

She had lost her composure, and couldn't get to sleep.

He was so dear to her.

But…

These aren't feelings of love.

They can't be love.

That person is my brother—she had told herself that ever since three years ago.

Three years ago, when that person saved me, and when I realized his true value… Even since then, I've done my best to become someone fitting for him to call his sister.

I've always hoped that one day I could help that person the same way he saved me. I still want nothing more than to become someone who is capable of helping him.

I don't desire anything from him.

My life should have already expired, and he saved me.

I may be nothing more than shackles binding him right now…

But one day, I want to be the key that sets him free.

I want to be useful to him.

——For the time being, that means making breakfast.

He could eat breakfast over there as well…

…but I know he'll politely leave some room and come back.

I'll have him eat a delicious breakfast.

Because that's what I can do right now.

Miyuki gave an energetic lunge and stood up, then stretched a long, high stretch.

[5]

Magic High School had many unique aspects, but its fundamental system didn't differ from normal schools.

There were club activities here at First High as well.

In order to be recognized by the school as an official club, you needed to have a certain number of members and achievements—this point was the same, too.

But for Magic High School, there were many clubs closely related to magic.

The nine high schools affiliated with the National Magic University would face off against one another in a certain major magical competition, and their results tended to reflect upon the images of each school. In terms of how much the school put into it, it might have been more than how much elite sports schools support traditional national sports. Clubs that achieved excellence during this battle, called the Nine School Competition, would gain many amenities, ranging from the club's budget going up to each individual member's standing within the school improving.

The contest to acquire promising new members was an important event, since it had a direct effect on a club's influence. The school not only recognized it but even seemed to actively encourage it.

Thus, the great struggle of all the clubs scrambling to gain new members reached its fiercest point at this time of year.

"...That all means clubs cause no end of trouble around this time."

The place: the student council room.

Tatsuya listened to Mari's explanation as he savored the taste of the bento Miyuki had made for him.

"Sometimes their solicitations are so extreme that it can obstruct classes. There is a specific time set up for these new student recruitment wars. It begins today and lasts for one week."

Those were the words of Mayumi, sitting next to Mari.

Miyuki was sitting next to Tatsuya, like always.

Suzune and Azusa were absent. They had been here yesterday because Mayumi had summoned them. Apparently, they normally ate lunch with their classmates.

In addition, Mari had brought a homemade bento again. Mayumi had been pretty grumpy being the only one eating a mechanically prepared meal from the dining server, but her mood finally seemed to have improved. She had declared that starting tomorrow, she'd make her own bento, too.

"During this time, the clubs are all going to put up invitation tents. It's not just your tiny, rural festival atmosphere. They'll all be scrambling to get their hands on anyone sneaking around who scored highly on the entrance exams, as well as the new students who have achievements in sports and things like that. Of course, there are rules—outwardly, anyway—and clubs that break them will be penalized by the club committee, but unfortunately it's not unusual for things to come to blows or even firefights in the shadows."

Tatsuya made a doubtful expression at what she said. "I thought we didn't permit students to carry around CADs."

You could still use magic without a CAD. But for things to evolve into anything as extreme as a firefight, you would basically need to use one.

Mari's answer baffled him.

"They have permission to use them for demonstrations for the new students. There are inspections here and there, but it's essentially a free pass. So during this time of year, the school ends up turning into a wild, lawless zone."

Well, yeah, of course it does, he thought reflexively. *Why would the school just let something like that slide...? Normally, they'd take measures to prevent it, like making inspections stricter.*

His next question was answered by Mayumi before he asked it.

"Even the school wants to win trophies at the Nine School Competition. That might be why they tolerate all the rules violations—to get more students into the clubs."

Compulsory participation in extracurricular activities had been banned by the competent ministry a few decades ago as a violation of the students' human rights. But the streets were brimming with students scouted for club activities, and realistically they overlooked sports scouting, using academic freedom of choice as a front for both, making it a self-contradictory and meaningless ban. But although it was just a front, it was effective enough that you couldn't just ignore it outright.

"Anyway, that's why the disciplinary committee will be on full alert for one week, starting today. Boy, am I glad we got a replacement member in time," she said, glancing to the side, probably sarcastically.

"Good for you for finding someone good, Mari!" Mayumi replied, warding the sarcasm off with a smile. Neither of them twitched an eyebrow—this sort of exchange must have been an everyday occurrence, all year round.

Tatsuya swallowed the last bite of his food, then put his chopsticks down. His teacup was filled back up from next to him. He took a sip of it and offered a measly resistance.

"Won't the clubs be targeting people with the best grades—so Course 1 students? I don't think I'll be very much help."

Mari had already declared her public stance that Course 2 students should be in control of other Course 2 students, so this statement was sabotage in disguise. But...

"Don't worry about it. You've got plenty of firepower to bring to the table."

...it was wholly dismissed.

Having been cut down from the front like that, there was nothing else to be said.

"...I see. Okay. We're patrolling after school, right?"

"Once your classes end, come to the HQ."

"All right," accepted Tatsuya obediently. It was an odd reaction, somewhere between being sportsmanlike and being too quick to give up.

Next to him, Miyuki looked to Mayumi for instruction. "President... Will we be included in keeping things in order?"

We meant the student council officers. Tatsuya felt content seeing that his sister, who was always a little moody in her interpersonal relationships despite being sociable on the surface, had already blended into the student council.

"I'll have Ah-chan help out the patrols. Hanzou and I need to be waiting in the club association room in case anything happens, so I want you and Rin to mind this place while we're gone."

"Understood," nodded Miyuki faithfully, but Tatsuya could tell she was a little disappointed. He hadn't thought she was the type that liked battle, but ability-wise there was no problem. Maybe she wanted to try out the new restraint-family techniques he'd inserted on her CAD.

Tatsuya, while misunderstanding that if he asked her she might cry out *No!* and then say something under her breath like ...*Tatsuya, you're stupid*, asked the question that immediately came to mind.

"Nakajou is going to be patrolling?"

The hidden emphasis was that Azusa wouldn't be reliable. It was another statement in disguise like before, but this time it was addressed, perhaps because someone else had done it.

"I can understand you being nervous about it because of how she looks. But you mustn't judge a book by its cover, Tatsuya."

"I understand that, but..." Tatsuya had actually been concerned about Azusa's timid personality. She must have immediately understood that vague part he'd tried to say. Mayumi, smiling, shook her head.

"She's a little—well, maybe a lot? Anyway, she's weak spirited, and that's the fly in the ointment, so to say. But Ah-chan's magic comes in really handy at times like these."

Mari made the same sort of dry smile. "You got that right. If we're talking about how good she is in situations where there's a huge uproar we can't settle down, there's no better magic than her Azusa Bow."

Modern magic was a technology—most magic had been formalized and shared. Of course, there were secret techniques as well, but the greater portion of magic was public and recorded in databases. Those spells were normally classified by family and effect, but highly original techniques were given their own names.

"Azusa Bow...? That's not an official nickname, is it? Is that outer magic?"

However, as far as Tatsuya knew, there was no public magic called Azusa Bow.

Many spells that weren't public were not of a family. Was it outer magic?

That had been what Tatsuya asked, but...

"...Are you saying you know literally every magic nickname?"

Instead of answering his question, Mari asked one in return, her voice astonished.

"...Tatsuya, are you actually linked up to a huge database from a satellite or something?"

Mayumi's eyes were wide, and she meant it.

Miyuki felt the urge to burst out into laughter at the responses of her upperclassmen, but this wasn't the first time she'd witnessed this kind of scene. She didn't have to try very hard to retain a modest expression.

In modern magic, which had its start as research into supernatural abilities, the phenomenon of magic was not analyzed and classified based on its outward appearance, such as "making fire" or "shooting wind," but rather by its function.

It was split into four families, each of which had two types:

❅ [Acceleration / Weighting]

❅ [Movement / Oscillation]

❅ [Convergence / Divergence]

❅ [Absorption / Emission]

Of course, exceptions exist to any system of classification, and there was magic that wasn't classifiable even in the four-family / eight-type schema of modern magic.

Magic that didn't belong to any of the four families were broadly separated into three categories.

The first was perception-type magic, which had been called ESP. (ESP, in this case, didn't refer to supernatural abilities as a whole but rather to the perception type.)

The second was magic that didn't alter events by temporarily overwriting the eidos, the information bodies accompanying those events—but rather magic with the objective of controlling the psions themselves. This was called typeless magic. Mayumi's specialty, firing clumps of psions, was the model example of typeless magic. The magic Tatsuya had used to knock Hattori out hadn't strictly been vibration family magic but typeless magic. However, there were spells in the form of psion manipulation that fell into one of the four families and eight types. The distinction between magic from one of the four families and typeless magic wasn't very sharp.

And the last was magic that dealt not with physical events but with mental phenomena. This was called outer magic. Outer magic was magic that wasn't part of any of the four families—it couldn't be classified as one. It spanned many things, from divine magic and spirit magic, which used spiritual things, to mind reading, ethereal separation, and consciousness control.

As if satisfied he'd shown normal surprise, Mayumi finally began to detail the Azusa Bow. "Like you guessed, Ah-chan's Azusa Bow is outer magic, of the emotional interference type. It has the effect of guiding all people in a specific area into a trancelike state."

Emotional interference–type magic was a subset of mental interference magic. Instead of affecting a person's thoughts or consciousness, it affected their impulses and emotions.

"The Azusa Bow doesn't make them fall unconscious, and it doesn't hijack their minds. It only causes them to fall into a state in which they can't oppose her. But it works on an entire area instead of just one person. So unlike most other mental interference–type spells, it can affect multiple people simultaneously. It's just the right magic to bring along for pacifying excited crowds!"

Tatsuya furrowed his brow upon hearing her supplementary explanation. "...Doesn't that sort of magic have class 1 restrictions on it...?"

The usage of outer magic was controlled more strictly than magic from the four families due to its oft-unique characteristics. Among them, the usage conditions for mental interference–type magic were particularly harsh.

Even just limited to the explanations given here, this magic could be used as a terrifying brainwashing tool. That was because people placed into a trance were much more open to suggestion.

If the existence of this magic was known, then the stream of dictatorial governments, terrorists, and cult leaders trying to use it would be endless.

When Tatsuya pointed that out, Mayumi smiled and told him not to worry.

"Can you really imagine Ah-chan being a dictator?"

"She could always be forced into cooperating."

"That's even less likely. She'd get all teary eyed just from picking up a few coins on the road. With her mental state, she'd be crushed by feelings of guilt, and then she wouldn't be able to use magic at all, right?"

The established theory—almost common sense at this point— was that magic was influenced by one's mental state.

If she had such a virtuous character, then just being aware that she was involved in the heavy crime of mass brainwashing could cause her to become unable to use magic.

Of course, if she was *extremely* timid, then one could always make her depend on them and then use her, but there was no need to pursue this train of thought any further.

There was a more general issue at hand.

"I believe the laws restricting mental interference–type magic apply no matter how good Nakajou's character may be..."

It was pointed out by Miyuki, and Mayumi struggled to find words.

"...Umm, that's okay, Miyuki. We don't let her use it outside school."

Her answer in desperation was incoherent.

She didn't seem the type to be weak when driven into a corner, but if Mari hadn't assisted her here, then she might have ended up in a pretty bad state.

"Mayumi... The way you say it will give them a considerable misunderstanding. Nakajou has special permission to use outer magic only if she's at school. It's a little trick—a loophole in the usage restrictions being looser for research organizations."

"I see."

"So there is that sort of method."

"Yes, that's right..."

Mayumi faked a smile at the Shiba siblings' nodding, convinced, at Mari's follow-up.

◇ ◇ ◇

Afternoon classes ended, and though he was reluctant, Tatsuya was about to head for the disciplinary committee room when a high-key voice stopped him.

He turned around to see the slender girl with short hair that wasn't too short. The term *sharp* might have been better than *slender* to describe her.

"Erika... That's unusual. Are you by yourself?"

"Is it? In my opinion, I'm not really the type to make many plans with people."

Now that she mentions it, she has a point, thought Tatsuya.

"Anyway, Tatsuya, what are you doing for a club? Mizuki already decided to join the art club. She invited me to do it with her, but I'm not really the artsy type. I'm just gonna wander around and see if there's anything interesting."

"Leo said he already decided, too, right?"

"Yeah, the mountaineering club. It suits him so well that it hurts."

"Well... It certainly does suit him."

"Our mountaineering club is apparently more keen on survival skills than mountain climbing. There's, like, nowhere else he could even be," Erika said under her breath in cursing, then gave a vaguely uninterested look. "Tatsuya, if you haven't decided on a club yet, want to come with me?"

If she'd said that to *him*, he would have gotten angry and denied her, but she had a slightly lonesome look on her face, and he couldn't refuse her.

"Actually, the disciplinary committee is putting me straight to work. We'd both be wandering around the place, but I'd have to be on patrol at the same time. If that's okay with you, then I'll come."

"Hmm. Well, all right, then. I guess we'll meet in front of the classroom."

Erika feigned self-importance as she thought about Tatsuya's invitation, then gestured reluctantly and answered.

Her smile, though, betrayed her act.

◇ ◇ ◇

"Why are you here?!"

That was the first thing Tatsuya heard at the beginning of his second encounter.

"Well, say whatever you like, but it's absurd."

Tatsuya's attitude, with his astounded voice and sigh, only invited yet more excitement.

"What was that?!"

This time, he looked like he might come over and grab him, rather than just sounding like it.

But…

"Quiet down, newbie!"

Roared at by Mari, Shun Morisaki hurriedly shut his mouth and straightened up even further.

"This is a business meeting of the disciplinary committee. Nobody present here is not of the disciplinary committee. Please, have at least a tiny bit of common sense to know that."

"I am sorry!"

Morisaki's face was pathetically drawn back with nervousness and fear.

Mari had only dragged him into this the day before yesterday. And even if that hadn't been the case, being reprimanded by someone with the same authority as the student president or club association chairman was a lot of responsibility for a new student. Especially for those who were too serious about it.

"Fine, just sit down."

Before the Course 1 student who was standing there, all the blood drained from his face, Mari ordered him to take his seat with an awkward expression.

When Tatsuya matched this with what he'd seen of her behavior from yesterday, she seemed to have the exact *opposite* personality of someone who took pleasure in abusing those with a lower rank than she had.

Morisaki took his seat across from Tatsuya. Neither of them wanted to be in this position, but they were the freshmen here. They were on the lowest rung. Having to stare at each other at the lowest seats on the table was unavoidable.

"Everyone's here, right?"

After that, the two seniors came in one after another, and when there were nine people in the room, Mari stood up.

"Just sit there and listen. This year's noisy week is right around the corner. This will be the disciplinary committee's first climax of the new year. There are those who got carried away and caused a huge problem last year—as well as those who so kindly made it worse for us by trying to calm it down—but this year, I want us all to put in our best efforts so that we don't have to deal with any problem children. I don't want any officers taking the initiative and causing issues, got it?"

After seeing more than one person wince, Tatsuya, who knew all too well he had a problem with getting into trouble, cautioned himself not to go down the same path.

"Thankfully, this year, our graduate replacements made it on time. I'll introduce them. Please stand."

They hadn't been warned in the briefing about this part, but they both promptly stood up, without difficulty or confusion.

Though there was a distinct difference in enthusiasm in their expressions.

Morisaki was standing at attention, without hiding, or even trying to hide, his nervousness, and instead that made him look enthusiastic. Tatsuya had the air of someone who wasn't quite taking this seriously enough, despite his calm countenance.

People who considered superiority important probably would prefer Morisaki's attitude, and for those who thought real strength was the most important, Tatsuya probably looked more reliable.

"This is Shun Morisaki from 1-A and Tatsuya Shiba from 1-E. They'll be joining us on patrol starting today."

A stir arose, and it was probably because of them hearing the class Tatsuya was from. He didn't hear the word *Weed* whispered, however—as expected from the headquarters of those who prevented the use of such slurs.

"Are we partnering up?"

It may not have been to deflect the issue, but a sophomore named Okada raised his hand and said that. He was one of the ones elected by the teachers.

"As I explained last time, for the week of the recruitment wars, you'll each be patrolling by yourself. The newbies are no exception to that."

"Will they help?"

Okada's question had been directed toward both Tatsuya and Morisaki for form's sake, but his gazing at Tatsuya's left breast spoke to what he really meant.

He had predicted this response, so he gave Mari a look that delegated it to her.

But he hadn't needed to delegate it. Mari gave Okada a bored, peeved look.

"Yeah, don't worry. They're both reliable. I've seen Shiba's skills with my own eyes, and Morisaki's device handling is nothing to make light of. He just went up against the wrong opponent the other day. If you're still concerned, then you can go with Morisaki."

Okada looked a little embarrassed at the casual reply, but he managed to keep his calm and reply with an "I'll pass" in a sarcastic tone.

"Anybody else have anything to say?"

Tatsuya was considerably surprised—Mari's voice certainly hadn't sounded gentle. In fact, it sounded like she was asking for a fight. Other than Morisaki and him, though, nobody seemed to be paying it any mind.

It must have been a frequent occurrence. It seemed there was some deep-rooted antagonism in the committee.

Tatsuya wondered, though, about the leader taking it upon herself to fan those flames.

"Let's move to the final briefing. Your patrol routes will be the same as the ones you've been briefed on before now. I don't expect there will be anyone opposed to it at this point."

The atmosphere didn't quite feel like there were no objections, but there was no one who assertively tried to argue.

"All right. Get to your routes immediately. Don't forget your recorders. I'll explain things to Shiba and Morisaki. Everyone else, move out!"

All present stood at once, put their feet together, and hit their left breasts with their right fists.

Tatsuya wondered what they were doing, but according to what he heard later, this was the salute adopted by all the disciplinary committee members of the past. In addition, there was apparently a rule for saying *Good morning* to her no matter what time of day it was.

The six people, excluding Mari, Tatsuya, and Morisaki, each went to leave the room, one after another. The fifth and sixth, Koutarou and Sawaki, told Tatsuya "not to get too far ahead of himself" and to "ask me if there's anything you're not sure about" (who said which is obvious), then left the room themselves.

He politely (at least, outwardly speaking) saw the two of them off. Morisaki glared at him bitterly.

Mari, watching them, somehow staved off a headache and a sigh, then addressed them.

"First, I'll give you these."

Mari gave them each, as they lined up side to side, an armband and a thin video recorder.

"Put the recorder in your jacket pocket. It's made to be just big enough so the lens sticks out. The switch is on the right side."

As she said, when he placed it in the chest pocket on his blazer, it was big enough to record something just like that.

"From here on, make sure to take your recorder with you whenever you go on patrol. If you spot any disorderly conduct, turn it on immediately. But you don't need to worry about the recording. As a general rule, the words of disciplinary committee officers are taken as proof. Just think of it more as a precaution."

She awaited their response, then directed them to take out their portable terminals.

"I'll send you the transmission code for the disciplinary committee… All right, check to make sure you have it."

The two of them reported that they had received it just fine.

"Make sure to use this code when you want to report something. And whenever we need to give you instructions, we'll use this code, so make sure it checks out.

"Lastly, about CADs. Disciplinary committee officers are permitted to carry CADs on school grounds. There's no need for you to get someone's permission to use them. But if it's discovered you used it improperly, you'll be given a much stricter punishment than normal students because you're a member of the disciplinary committee. There was someone who got expelled because of it the year before last, too. Don't make light of it."

"I have a question."

"I'll allow it."

"May we use the disciplinary committee's CADs?"

Tatsuya's question must have been pretty unexpected, because there was a short pause before she gave a reply.

"…I don't mind, but what's your reason? I may be preaching to the choir here, but those are older models, you know."

Mari had guessed by his handling of them before and after the match yesterday, as well as him maintaining the room, that he was fairly skilled when it came to CADs.

And she also knew because of Azusa's spiel that his own CAD was a high-spec variety.

And yet he was telling her that he wanted to use old ones instead.

She couldn't suppress her curiosity.

"They may be old models, but they're still high-end items made for experts," he answered with a wry grin. Sure enough, she hadn't even thought about that.

"...Are they?"

"Yes. That series is infamous for being a pain to adjust, but they have a high freedom of setting, and the sensitivity of their noncontact switches is superior. There are people who are wildly enthusiastic about maintaining them. Whoever purchased them must have been a big fan. If you ignore the fact that it makes the battery life shorter, you can overclock them so that their processing speed is on par with the newest models. If you brought it to the right place, they would fetch a fairly high price."

"...And we were treating them like garbage, is that it? *Now* I see why you were being so insistent on cleaning them up."

"I feel like Nakajou would know about that model series as well..."

"Nakajou is too scared to come down here."

"Ha-ha..."

The two of them exchanged wry grins.

Then Mari finally realized that Morisaki was being left out.

"Ahem. You can use them freely if you wish. They've been doing nothing but collecting dust, after all."

"Then...I'll borrow these two."

"Two...? You really are interesting."

Tatsuya picked up the two CADs he'd quietly copied his adjustment data onto yesterday. Mari saw him and grinned, and Morisaki's lips curled into an expression of distaste.

◇ ◇ ◇

"Hey."

Right after Mari left them to go to the club association room, Morisaki called out to Tatsuya from behind. Tatsuya could tell by his tone he didn't want to say anything friendly. He thought more than half seriously about outright ignoring him, but he figured that would make his problems worse, so he reluctantly turned around.

"What?" he responded insolently, his hostility on full display—there was no reason to come off as friendly right now.

"Looks like bluffing is your specialty. Did you bluff your way past the president and chairwoman like that?"

"Are you jealous?"

"Wha…?"

If that's all it takes to get you distracted, then don't start stuff like this in the first place, thought Tatsuya. On the other hand, Morisaki's honesty was enviable.

"…But you went too far this time. There's no way a Course 2 kid like you could ever use more than one CAD."

He listened to Morisaki speak. Morisaki hadn't called him a Weed, but Tatsuya cynically thought that was probably only because he knew Tatsuya was on the disciplinary committee. Morisaki didn't notice Tatsuya's apathetic expression, however, and continued to lecture proudly, as if intoxicated by his own words.

"If you equip a CAD in both hands, you won't be able to use either because of the psionic interference. You were trying to look cool, but you didn't even know that simple thing, did you? You can't even use real magic anyway. You just sneak around so that you don't embarrass yourself."

"Was that supposed to be advice? You've got a lot of free time, Morisaki."

"Hah! I'm different from all of you. You may have taken me by surprise the other day, but I won't screw up again. I'll show you the difference between you and us."

As Tatsuya watched him leave after saying that, he thought about how nice it must be to believe that there *would* be a next time…

◇ ◇ ◇

Despite having made plans with Tatsuya, Erika wasn't outside the classroom.

I don't particularly mind, but…

Tatsuya heaved another sigh—which had already become a habit since school started—and booted up the LPS on his portable terminal.

It displayed a map of the school grounds and a red blip moving slowly through it.

It meant that she had the consideration not to shut the power down on her terminal.

She hadn't gone very far yet.

I had this set up just in case something happened, but…

She was counting on him to come looking for her.

He zoomed in on the display, specified her position, then began to walk toward the signal being emitted by Erika's terminal.

The cluster of tents, which looked from the window like they were burying the entire schoolyard, and even the roads in between school buildings, looked just like stalls at a fair.

"Just like a festival…" murmured Erika to herself. Upon realizing she had, she was almost overcome with the urge to grin at herself.

She'd always been alone more frequently than not.

But ever since school here started, that tendency had vanished.

Being by myself is unusual, huh… You don't actually have a very good eye for girls, do you, Tatsuya? she said in her mind's eye to the boy that she—not he—had stood up.

In junior high school, and even during elementary school, being alone was the status quo for her.

It wasn't because she didn't like people or anything. She was a relatively sociable person—she could get along with anyone pretty quickly.

But in exchange, they would soon find themselves neglected.

She wasn't able to be with someone around the clock and go with them everywhere.

She had analyzed herself, saying that she had a weak attachment to personal relationships.

Friends she had been relatively close to said they were disillusioned.

They said she was like a fickle cat.

One friend she broke up with even called her arrogant and haughty.

The stream of boys following her about never ended, but none stayed for very long, either.

Free, unrestrained, unfettered by promises—that was her motto.

…Well, it was, anyway… Maybe I've been acting kind of strange lately.

Looking at it objectively, she felt that lately, she'd been hanging around *him* quite a bit.

Just a little while ago, it would have been inconceivable for *her* to ask *him* to come with her.

But it was only the first week, she thought, so maybe she'd get tired of him like she always did.

At the same time, it felt different from the way it always did…

"Erika?"

Ten minutes from the agreed-upon time.

As Erika was just exiting the school building to go into the yard, she heard Tatsuya's voice calling her.

He caught up pretty fast, she thought.

"Tatsuya, you're late."

"…Sorry."

She saw a momentary scowl flash across his face, but he seemed to be immediately convinced by something, and he meekly bowed his head.

"…You're apologizing?" It was contrary to her expectations, and instead, Erika was the one confused by it.

"It was only ten minutes, but it is past the time I agreed on, after all. Me being late and you not being where we agreed are separate issues, right?"

"Ack... Sorry."

It was a somewhat strange expression, but he smiled at her, deathly serious, and Erika wasn't even able to get a retort in.

"...Hey, Tatsuya, do you get told that you have a bad personality?"

"That was unexpected. I've never had anyone complain about my personality. I've been told I'm bad with people, though."

"That's the same thing! It might even be worse!"

"Oh, my mistake. It wasn't that I'm bad with people; it was that I'm a bad person."

"And that's *definitely* worse!"

"I've been called a demon before, too."

"All right already!"

Before Erika's ragged breathing, and with the air of pondering a profound philosophical problem, Tatsuya bent his head to the side.

"You seem quite tired. Are you all right?"

"...Tatsuya, you've definitely been told you have a bad personality."

"Actually, I have."

"Was all that a lie?!"

Erika hung her head dejectedly.

◇ ◇ ◇

It took a bit to improve her mood, but he managed to do it before he drew any odd stares—and before she drew any observatory glances or jeering stares—and returned to his patrol.

And he wanted to leave within five minutes.

He had no choice but to admit he'd underestimated this business. —Not admit to anyone in particular, though.

In all honesty, he had made light of it, thinking that despite Mari using the term *chaos*, it was still only high school clubs trying to recruit people. But it was nowhere near that simple.

Now that he'd seen it, he fully understood the need for people to control it. Even ten people or so wouldn't have been enough for this.

Between the tents filling up the schoolyard, a crowd had formed. Beyond the crowd was a wailing Erika, who could no longer escape. Her demeanor was fairly smart, too, but she couldn't seem to oppose violence in numbers. …Though Tatsuya himself was acting as though he had promptly slipped away and was watching from afar, so he didn't quite have room to talk.

Of course, he could hardly say with finality that this outcome meant that Tatsuya was quicker on his feet than Erika. That was because compared to him, Erika was being targeted by overwhelming numbers of people.

Tatsuya was on the taller side for a new student, but he was on the thin side. At a glance, he seemed boring, and his eyes were sharp, but not sharp enough to stand out very much. Add to that the fact that he was a Course 2 student, and not many people had their eyes on him for recruitment.

On the other hand, Erika was pretty enough to stand out quite a bit. And in contrast to beauties like Miyuki, to whom people would hesitate to touch with their hand, let alone make a move on her, Erika was the type where you wanted to reach out for her even though you knew you'd get burned.

The long and short of what happened was…

…that Erika was being swarmed with club recruitment offers.

The fact that she was a Course 2 student presented no obstacle in this case. (Though Erika would say that it wasn't helping her at all.)

They were most likely looking for a mascot or a billboard character, and the ones waging war over her were mostly nonmagic sports and exercise clubs.

She was at the center, and they were swallowing her up.

Tatsuya couldn't see what was happening on the inside of the crowd—but they were probably grabbing her shoulders and pulling on her arms, or clinging to her from behind in a scramble for their *prey* in behavior that, even if they were the same gender, would still be construed as sexual harassment. He could guess that things were reaching a point where he couldn't let it go once he got an almost *bloodthirsty* feeling drifting from it.

But Erika was more persevering than he thought. Tatsuya had escaped on his own—abandoning her in the process—because he figured she'd be able to force her way out pretty quickly.

You couldn't hold Erika down just because you did a little bit of regular physical activity. Tatsuya had no doubts about that. The skill with which she had knocked away Morisaki's CAD was certainly not something a freshman or sophomore could learn.

The ones directly swarming her were female upperclassmen. He wasn't surprised that there were no rude male students trying to get their hands all over a girl's body. Even if they were one or two years older, Erika's strength would make it simple to break free of girls' arms and run away—at least, that was what he had predicted. Unfortunately, their being weak girls appeared to be working against her. Erika had decided not to use more violent methods against them.

But just as he was thinking he should probably go and get her out of there, he heard her voice.

"Hey, watch where you're touching! St-stop...!"

What he heard was, though lacking a bit of seductiveness, definitely Erika's scream.

It looked like things had gotten too real to be a joke anymore.

Tatsuya manipulated the CAD on his left arm, and as soon as he finished preparing the magic program, he kicked off the ground.

The ground shook—of course, it was far more than the vibrations that could be created by his own kick.

That vibration amplified the magic program he had formulated and gave it a vector.

The vibrations transmitted from the soles of their feet to their bodies wouldn't be enough to make them pass out. He couldn't fire such powerful magic with his strength.

But their bodies were shaken from underfoot, and the students

forming the crowd lost their sense of equilibrium without even realizing it.

Tatsuya plunged into the throng.

The upperclassmen who he pushed through easily fell onto their
backs.

He shoved his way through both boys and girls and reached the
center of the crowd without much trouble.

He split through the final wall made up entirely of female
students—

found the person he was looking for—

and grabbed hold of her arm.

"Run!"

That was all he said before he pulled Erika's left hand and dashed
away.

◇ ◇ ◇

Pushing his way—no, slipping like magic—through the crowd, Tatsuya escaped into the shadows of the schoolyard.

He let go of Erika's hand, which had been connected to his, looked
back, and that was when he finally noticed the disastrous situation she
was in. Her hair was badly tousled, one of the sides of her blazer was
practically coming off, her brand-new uniform was all wrinkled, and
she held her completely untied necktie in her right hand.

With the necktie disconnected, the breast of the uniform was
exposing her ever so slightly. She must have been holding it down
while they were running, but just as she looked down a bit to fix her
clothes—that was when Tatsuya's gaze happened to look that way.

"Don't look!"

She probably noticed that he'd turned around when her down-
turned eyes glimpsed the direction of his feet. Erika spoke immediately, but just before being yelled at, Tatsuya had already averted his
face and body.

"…Did you see?" Erika asked, her voice making it easy to imagine how red her face was.

"……" But Tatsuya couldn't immediately devise an answer for her.

He should probably say he didn't see anything. That would be the smart way to handle this.

However…

Her chest, ever so slightly tanned and yet still retaining its original paleness.

The distinct lines of her collarbone.

Even the beige color of the lace decorating the edges of her bra had been burned into his memory.

"Did you see?"

The sound of clothes rustling had ceased, so he deduced she was finished fixing herself.

At the same time, the change in her tone of voice told Tatsuya that his moratorium had expired.

Now that it came to this, he should at least let her punch him one time. Even if he bore no fault at all, he needed to show that sincerity—as a man.

—As he had such escapist thoughts (because he couldn't say he was completely without fault. At the least, he was at fault for leaving her there in the first place) Tatsuya slowly turned around.

Thankfully, there was no voice stopping him. If she still hadn't finished getting her clothes in order, improving the situation would become hopeless.

He saw Erika, whose collar was buttoned all the way up, and her necktie was tightly around her neck, and secretly felt relieved. Come to think of it, if she'd had it buttoned all the way up to begin with, things might not have ended up so disastrous. Tatsuya thought that having compromised herself by undoing her top button and loosening her necktie had made the damage worse.

But he only thought that—he didn't say it.

"I saw. I'm sorry."

There was no way he could say it when faced with the red hue lingering around her eyes.

Erika glared harshly up at him. Her cheeks reddened again, probably because her embarrassment had come back. Her clenched fist was trembling, probably because she was enduring her shame.

"…Stupid!"

Her hand didn't come flying at him. Instead, he took a hit right to the shin.

Erika kicked him in the leg, then spun around to turn away from him.

She began to briskly walk away. Tatsuya followed her without a word.

He couldn't see from here, but she was probably tearing up.

His shins were so built that they could withstand an oaken sword hitting them.

Her boots were made of a flexible material, and not even strengthened at the toes, so she doubtlessly hurt herself more. But if he showed any consideration for that, it would only invite further attacks.

He had his hands full just trying to pretend not to notice her unnatural gait.

◇ ◇ ◇

Although tents filled the schoolyard to capacity, that was just the schoolyard—in the exclusive fields, the clubs that normally used them were putting on demonstrations.

It was the same in the gymnasiums.

When they walked over to the second small gymnasium, nicknamed the arena, they found the kendo club giving a martial arts demonstration.

—Erika's head had long since cooled down. She'd known from the start that she was just venting. The fact that Tatsuya never said a word to try to excuse himself had produced results. Although he did think it was too soon for her to mumble "It's so humid" and loosen her necktie and undo her topmost button again in order to battle the heat.

The two of them looked down on the kendo demo from the observation area set up in the hallway three meters up the wall of the small gymnasium.

"Hmm... So there's a kendo club, even though this is a magic high school," said Erika casually to herself.

"Doesn't every school have at least a kendo club?" asked Tatsuya, also casually. Actually, maybe it wasn't a question so much as an idle statement to keep the conversation going.

But Erika stared at his face fixedly for no short period of time.

"...What?"

"...I'm surprised."

"At what?"

"That there was something even you didn't know. And most people experienced in martial arts know, too."

Tatsuya got a little worried upon hearing Erika's remark. "Do I really look like a know-it-all?"

"Huh? Um, no, not that. It's just, you have that kind of air about you, like you know everything."

"That kind of air? ...I'm a freshman like you, Erika. Well, whatever. Anyway, why are kendo clubs unusual?"

"R-Right. We are both freshmen... It feels a little weird to call us alike, though... Umm, so about kendo clubs. Magicians and people who want to be magicians almost never do kendo at the high school level. Instead of kendo, magicians use *kenjutsu*, which has sword techniques that incorporate spells. There are a lot of kids who practice kendo up until around elementary school to learn the basics, but the kids who decide they want to be a magician during junior high school pretty much all drift over to *kenjutsu*."

"Huh, I see... I had thought kendo and *kenjutsu* were the same thing."

"I'm really surprised!" said Erika.

"Tatsuya, you look like you have so much skill in martial arts that use weapons, and yet... Oh, I got it!"

"What's the matter?" This time Tatsuya was surprised—why was she suddenly raising her voice like that?

And Tatsuya wasn't the only one paying attention to her now that she did that so suddenly, but Erika herself didn't notice it. She answered his question with a face that said she understood and an expression that said it made sense.

"Tatsuya, you're thinking that incorporating magic into weapon techniques is just what you're supposed to do, don't you? No, maybe it's not only magic. Fighting spirit, and prana, and stuff like that—you think you're just supposed to complement physical techniques with them, don't you?"

"Are you *not* supposed to? You're muscles aren't the only thing that moves your body, are they?"

From Tatsuya's point of view, what Erika had said was abrupt and obvious.

Erika nodded to herself at his reply and response. "It may seem totally natural to you, but...for normal athletes, that's not how it goes."

"I see."

That was an indirect way of saying it, but Tatsuya finally realized that there seemed to be a gap between his knowledge and common sense.

"By the way, maybe we should settle down soon and observe?"

This time it was Tatsuya's turn to make Erika understand the gap in her awareness.

She followed his meaningful gaze and finally noticed that the volume of her voice was drawing attention to herself.

Erika gave an ingratiating smile and silently looked down at the floor.

The first-stringers' exhibition match was quite impressive.

Among them, he took particular notice of a sophomore girl's demonstration.

She wasn't very big, even for a girl—her build was about the same as Erika's—but she was fighting evenly with bigger male students twice her size.

She didn't use power. Instead, she was parrying their strikes with flowing technique.

And it seemed like she still had more energy left.

Tatsuya thought that she was the perfect good-looking sword fighter to use in an exhibition match.

Most of the spectators found their gazes stolen by her skills.

But here, too, there was an exception.

And right next to him, at that.

At the same time the girl delivered a brilliant strike *that looked staged* and bowed to her opponent…

He heard a dissatisfied snort from beside him.

"You don't like this very much, do you?"

"Huh? Yeah…"

She didn't appear to immediately realize she was being asked something, so there was a moment before Erika's reply came.

"…I mean, look at how boring it is. She knows exactly what her inferior opponent has, and she acts all tough and spaces herself out, and then takes the point, as planned. It's not a match. It's just a staged fight."

"Well, you're right, but…" Tatsuya naturally began to smile. "It's to advertise, so isn't that normal? There are a lot of pro athletes famous for *putting on* real sword battles, but a seriously real sword battle wouldn't be something to *show* to others, right? A real battle between experts is essentially a death match."

"…You're pretty calm."

"Aren't you just too worked up?"

Erika turned away from him, her face displeased.

But that expression of hers was a sort of show itself.

Erika probably thought of her ostentatious movements and spacing neglected the true art, that it was dishonest—and she was angry about it.

But when Tatsuya pointed it out, she seemed to get even angrier.

She probably wouldn't ever barge in on them, but she could possibly do something close to it. Tatsuya decided to ward that possibility off and urged Erika to come out with him.

Or rather, he *tried* to.

Right after they had left the observation zone and approached the entrance to the gymnasium, a stir of a different sort than canvassing came to them from behind.

They couldn't hear it very well, but they knew people where arguing over something.

He looked beside him, and Erika looked back up at him. Her eyes were brimming with curiosity.

The first one to force their way through the ring of steadily-getting-more-excited people was Erika. Tightly gripping Tatsuya's sleeve.

Tatsuya, too, approached the center of the clamor, pulled along by Erika.

People frowned at them as they split through the crowd—the power of Erika's insincere smile was a big reason they didn't get into a fight over it—and they managed to make it to a spot where they could see what was happening.

They saw a male sword fighter and a female sword fighter confronting each other.

The girl was the one from the duel before—in Erika's words, the one who was staging the fight. Her body armor was still on, but her helmet was off. She was fairly pretty, with semilong, straight black hair that left an impression. With her skills and her looks, she was probably the perfect person to draw in new members.

"Hmm. Tatsuya, you like people like her?"

"No, I think you're cuter."

"...It doesn't make me happy when you say it monotone like that."

As she glared at him displeased, the skin around her upturned eyes was tinged with red.

"I'm not used to it."

"…Geez!" She continued to mumble about something or other, but she didn't seem to want to take further issue with it, so Tatsuya moved on to the boy.

He wasn't that big—probably smaller than Tatsuya—but his whole body was lean, like a coiled spring. He was holding a *shinai*, the bamboo sword used in kendo, but in any case he didn't have any armor on.

Tatsuya considered grabbing someone nearby and asking them what was going on, but there was no need.

"There's still more than an hour until the *kenjutsu* club's turn, Kirihara! Why can't you wait that long?"

"I'm surprised, Mibu. You can't show the greatest strengths of the kendo club to newcomers playing with novices like these. I just thought I'd help you out a bit!"

"You forced your way in here to pick a fight?! I can't believe you just used the word *help*. If the disciplinary committee knew about the violence you displayed toward your upperclassman, it wouldn't just be your problem anymore."

"Violence? Hey, now, Mibu. People are gonna misunderstand. He was wearing armor *and* I used a *shinai*. I just knocked him in the face a bit. Even if he had been a kendo club regular, it's nothing to get your panties in a bunch over. And he was the one who attacked first, remember?"

"That's because *you* provoked him!"

The blades of their words pierced into each other. He'd thought they might not say any more, but each conveniently responded to the other's questions.

"This is getting interesting," muttered Erika, half to herself and half not. He could tell from her tone of voice that she was excited. "This fight would be way more interesting than that farce earlier."

"Do you know those two?"

"Well, I've never met them in person," she answered immediately.

She must not have been talking to herself after all. "I just remembered I've seen the girl in a match before. Sayaka Mibu. The year before last, she won second place at the national junior high school girl's kendo tournament. Everyone was calling her stuff like the 'gorgeous swordswoman' and the 'kendo belle.'"

"...But she got second."

"Well, the champion was... Well, not as photogenic."

"I see." Well, that was just how the media worked.

"The boy is Takeaki Kirihara. He was the champion of the Kanto Junior High School *kenjutsu* tournament two years ago. He got first place for real."

"Didn't he go to the nationals?"

"They only have national *kenjutsu* tournaments starting in high school. There wouldn't be nearly as many people before that."

Tatsuya nodded in understanding and agreement.

Kenjutsu was a sport that combined sword techniques with magical ones, so the athletes would need to use magic as a prerequisite.

Although advances in magic studies had brought forth the development of devices to aid in casting magic, only maybe one out of a thousand junior high school students, per grade, would be able to activate magic at a practical level.

And those who could maintain that magical power at a practical level even after maturing would be less than a tenth of that.

Course 2 students were treated as leftovers inside this school, but compared to the overall population, they were elites, too.

"Whoops, looks like they're starting soon."

Tatsuya was also feeling that the string of tension was reaching its breaking point.

Preparing for the worst, he got the armband out of his pocket and put it on his left arm. Students nearby looked at him, surprised, and their eyes widened again upon seeing the absence of the school crest on his left breast, but Tatsuya was paying attention only to the two confronting each other.

The female student must have been hesitant to strike at an opponent who wasn't wearing armor. But as long as they were pointing their words at each other and not stepping down, a clash of swords was unavoidable.

The boy—Kirihara—would probably make the first move.

"Don't worry about it, Mibu. This is a kendo club demonstration. I'll do you a favor and not use magic."

"You think you have a chance with just sword skills? The *kenjutsu* club uses magic like a cane, but the kendo club has only been polishing its sword skills."

"Those are some big words, Mibu. Then I'll let you see it! I'll show you the *kenjutsu* techniques that let us compete on another level past physical limitations!"

That was the signal to start.

Kirihara suddenly swung his *shinai* down at her uncovered head.

The two shinai violently rang against each other.

The yelps from the crowd came two beats later.

The onlookers probably didn't know what was happening.

They could only imagine how fierce the sword attacks the combatants were exchanging must be from the violent noises of *shinai* slamming together, which occasionally even had a metallic ring to them.

—Save for a few exceptions.

"Her kendo was pretty high level. If she was second, how amazing must first be?" Tatsuya exhaled in admiration of their sword skills—notably Sayaka's.

"No… She's like a different person than the Sayaka Mibu I saw. I can't believe she's gotten so much better in just two years…" answered Erika, taken by astonishment but also giving off a somehow bellicose air, as if she was hiding her face and licking her lips.

The two of them disengaged, their game of tug-of-war stopped for a moment, and each jumped backward to create distance between them.

The observers' responses were split: those who were breathing, and those who weren't.

"I wonder who'll win..." wondered Erika under her breath.

"Mibu has the advantage, right?" replied Tatsuya with a whisper.

"Why do you say that?"

"Kirihara is avoiding striking her in the face. It was a bluff, one which anticipated taking the first attack. They're not far enough apart for him to win when he's both not allowed to use magic and putting another handicap on himself. Even in a fair fight, if it was just a *shinai* duel, I think the odds would be in Mibu's favor."

"I mostly agree. But how long can Kirihara endure this?"

He couldn't have heard Erika's remark, but...

"Uohhhhh!"

...for the first time in the battle, Kirihara charged in with a war cry.

Each of them swung straight down.

"Hitting each other?"

"No, they're not even!"

Kirihara's *shinai* caught Sayaka's left upper arm...

...and Sayaka's *shinai* was planted in Kirihara's right shoulder.

"Kuh!"

Kirihara struck Sayaka's *shinai* aside with his left hand and took a big jump backward.

"Defeated because he changed his aim halfway through."

"I see—that's why his stance loosened. It was the perfect timing for a double hit...but in the end, he couldn't find it in him to do it."

Tatsuya and Erika weren't the only ones who saw that the duel was over.

The faces of the kendo club members looked relieved.

And the members of the *kenjutsu* club, the group that had made its way to the front of the gallery at some point, and wearing different uniforms than the kendo club, were making sour faces.

"If these were real swords, you'd be dead. You wouldn't have even reached my bones. Admit your defeat." Sayaka declared her victory, her expression dignified.

Kirihara scowled at her. Had he admitted that she was correct as a swordsman though his emotions tried to deny it?

"Hah, ha-ha-ha…" Kirihara broke out into a hollow laugh. Had he admitted his defeat?

It didn't look like it.

The water level of Tatsuya's internal danger sense suddenly shot up.

Sayaka, who was still facing him, probably understood the threat more distinctly than he did.

She readied her sword again, pointed the tip right at him, and glared sharply at Kirihara.

"If these were real swords? My body hasn't been cut at all! Mibu, you want a fight with **real swords**? Then…as you wish! I'll take you on for real!"

Kirihara took his right hand off his *shinai* and pressed it on his left wrist.

There was a scream from the onlookers.

The spectators covered their ears from the unpleasant noise that sounded like nails on glass.

There were a few who paled and fell to their knees, too.

Kirihara jumped in closer and swung his *shinai* down with his left hand.

Though his one-handed attack was swift, it didn't have the foremost power.

But Sayaka didn't take the attack—she leaped far backward.

It hadn't hit her.

It had grazed her, at most.

And yet there was a thin line across Sayaka's armor. It was the trace of where the *shinai* had grazed.

He had used a vibration-type close-combat spell called High-Frequency Blade to give his *shinai* the edge of a real sword.

"How is it, Mibu? This is a **real sword**!"

Once again, he swung his sword down at Sayaka with one hand.

And before his eyes, Tatsuya got in the middle of them.

Just before he jumped in, Tatsuya had lightly crossed his left and right arms, with CADs on them, and sent psions into them.

The tightly bound psionic stream—he imagined pressing the CADs' keys with psionic fingers.

By using the noncontact switch, the CADs outputted an activation program.

In a flash, the psionic wave itself, having been converted into an intricate pattern—the typeless magic was fired from Tatsuya.

This time, there were those among the onlookers who had to cover their mouths.

Symptoms not unlike motion sickness chained radically.

But in return, the unpleasant, high-pitched noise disappeared.

Kirihara's *shinai* and Tatsuya's arm crossed.

There was no sound of bamboo striking flesh.

What resonated was the sound of something falling to the wooden floor.

And then, what the observers saw, having been liberated from the noise and instability, having finally regained the ability to look and see what was happening…

…was Tatsuya grabbing the left wrist of Kirihara—who had been knocked away and thrown onto his back—and then pressing down on his shoulder with his knee.

◇ ◇ ◇

Hostile whispers broke the silence in the small gymnasium—in the arena.

"Who's that?" "I've never seen him before." "Isn't he a new student?" "Look, he's a Weed." "Why's a substitute getting involved?" "But that armband…" "Come to think of it, I heard the disciplinary committee chose a Course 2 freshman." "Seriously? A Weed in the disciplinary committee?"

The unrest was spreading with the *kenjutsu* club's position at its center.

Both boys and girls were whispering about him.

Half of the circling crowd of people launched unfriendly stares at Tatsuya.

The other half was holding its breath.

Being oppressed by an overwhelming away-game atmosphere, Tatsuya, still holding Kirihara down, took out his portable terminal's voice communication unit. His calm expression didn't seem like a bluff, at least as far as anyone could tell. His bearing resembled the bad guy—used to being booed at.

"—This is the second gymnasium. I've arrested one person. He's wounded, so please bring a stretcher just in case."

He hadn't said it very loudly, but his words reached the edges of the throng.

After a moment, right when what that meant sank in, one of the members of the *kenjutsu* club in the front row shouted angrily at him, confused.

"Hey, what's the meaning of this?!"

He'd probably lost his head. His question didn't really mean anything. Or maybe it wasn't a question, but a threat.

"I am asking for Kirihara to come with me, because he used magic improperly."

Tatsuya responded to his angry voice with honesty. ——Although his gaze remained fixed on the disabled Kirihara. He hadn't looked up, so while his answer might have been honest, it was hard to call it polite.

Depending on how you looked at it, it was making fun of him.

That was how the upperclassman in the *kenjutsu* club thought.

"Hey, you bastard! Don't give me that shit, you Weed!"

He reached his hands out to Tatsuya's collar.

Tatsuya let go of Kirihara and, still half down, slid backward.

He kept his eye on Kirihara, who had fallen down to the floor, his legs and back stretched out.

He must have felt pretty hazy to fail to fall gracefully when flung away like that. There wouldn't be any concern of him getting away like this. So judging, Tatsuya finally directed his eyes toward the upperclassman who had flared up at him (and was still flared up at him, in the present tense).

In response to Tatsuya's attitude—he seemed not even to be paying attention to him—the *kenjutsu* club member facing Tatsuya was grating his teeth with such force he thought he could hear the grinding.

Support fire from the crowd. "Why just Kirihara? Isn't Mibu from the kendo club guilty of the same crime? Both parties are to blame here!"

Of course, it was the support for Kirihara and the *kenjutsu* club member who had tried to grab Tatsuya, and criticism toward Tatsuya.

In response, Tatsuya answered in a level tone, again honestly. "I believe I said it was because of improper use of magic."

Erika, staggered, gave him a look that told him he should have just ignored them. Then, the thing that she feared happened.

"Bullshit!"

The upperclassman, now in a complete frenzy, went to grab Tatsuya again.

He swiveled his body like a matador to flee from his hands.

——But all that did was fan the flames.

This time he came at him with a fist, but once again, Tatsuya dodged it.

The *kenjutsu* club member madly threw punch after punch, but he was clearly out of his element when it came to empty-handed combat, and so his movements were sloppy. He may have been in a frenzy, but it didn't take someone of Tatsuya's skills to be able to easily dodge him.

He continued to evade the wide punches with light steps until their positions had reversed. The upperclassman, tired of getting nothing but air, stopped, and Tatsuya stopped with him—and just then...

A second *kenjutsu* club member came out of the crowd and rushed at Tatsuya's back.

His stance, with his arms stuck out oddly—was he going for a full nelson?

Erika tried to shout *Look out!* but before the words came out...

Tatsuya's body swung around.

His outstretched arm drew an arc through the air and swallowed up the body coming to grab him.

The second *kenjutsu* member collided with the first one, and the two of them rolled spectacularly to the ground in a pile.

Silence visited them again.

All noise had disappeared from the arena. No one even coughed.

But if veins popping out of people's heads made a noise, it would have been piercing the eardrums of Tatsuya and Erika right now.

In the next moment...

...the *kenjutsu* club members all charged Tatsuya at once.

There was a scream.

Everyone besides the *kenjutsu* club—not only the gallery, but even the kendo club members as well—scattered like spiderlings, afraid of being caught up in the brawl.

Among them, only one person, Sayaka—who could be said to be the cause of this incident—readied her stance, probably about to charge in and lend Tatsuya her support.

"Wait, Mibu!"

But a senior male member of the same club grabbed her arm and stopped her.

"Ah, Captain Tsukasa..."

She tried to resist for a moment, but when she saw the face of the person grabbing her arm, she obediently pulled back and left with him.

Her face was filled with guilt, but even still, she didn't bat away the hand of this senior—the captain of the boy's kendo team, Kinoe Tsukasa.

As Sayaka was dragged away from the brawl by the boy's captain, Tatsuya became the focus, and he met the attacks of the *kenjutsu* club members. However, in meeting the attacks, he didn't counter them—he continued to handle the Blooms by sidestepping and dodging them all.

His carriage was more steady than splendid—or perhaps the term *reliable* would have been best here. He only moved exactly as much as he needed to. He *had* to have known the precise order of the attacks of the upperclassmen, who were coming at him from all directions. He wasn't making a show out of it, dodging everything by just a hair, but rather he slipped past them with enough room to get himself out of danger. As part of his coordinated attempt to hold them all here, he would fake attacks and cause allies to hit each other, or become a wall and expertly wheel around to the outside in an arc, out of the way of opponents closing in on him. Despite ten people attacking him, the *kenjutsu* club couldn't even get him out of breath much less stop him from moving around.

Not a fragment of haste or unrest showed on his face. Not a scrap of sloppiness or stagnation showed in his movements. The disrespectful Weed didn't counterattack, not because he could not but because there was no need. He was making these *kenjutsu* club Blooms come to terms with that fact.

In the back of the group, a furious, red-faced *kenjutsu* club member tried to fire magic at Tatsuya. The leftover psionic light shining one after another must have meant that he had expanded an activation program and tried to use a spell.

However, his magic never went off.

Whenever Tatsuya directed his gaze there, along with tremors that brought forth nausea as if by motion sickness, the clumps of psions that couldn't form a magic program fizzled out into the empty air.

As they cursed angrily, their faces betraying their incomprehension, they again came at Tatsuya and tried to grab him and punch him, continuing to only hit air.

Sayaka didn't realize until the end that the boy's captain was watching this all with great interest.

To be continued

Afterword

Nice to meet you all. My name is Tsutomu Sato. Thank you very much for reading this book.

The Irregular at Magic High School is my debut work, corrected and revised from the serial version I began putting up on an Internet novel submission site in October 2008. Receiving the good fortune to publish something like this that I wrote purely for fun began with a single e-mail from the website's administrator.

It was a forward of an e-mail from ASCII Media Works, and in it was an invitation—a request for a meeting to discuss publication.

I honestly doubted my own eyes.

Novels are my biggest hobby. I love both writing and reading them for pleasure. So I had known before that I would like to reveal my works as a novelist in the arena of physical books. Once, as a side thing from my dead-end salaryman job, I submitted a novel I'd written in my free time to a publisher's new author award contest. But I thought to myself—this *The Irregular at Magic High School* was the sort of thing that would only be accepted as an amateur work on the free Internet. Wasn't it a bit *adventurous* for a big-name publishing company to handle?

Those were the things I was thinking—it would never work.

In reality, the publication company I'm referring to was ASCII

Media Works, and it was for the Sixteenth Dengeki Novel Award, but the work I submitted was rejected outright. If you'll forgive me for sounding like a poor loser, I had to compress the work's contents by 50 percent to meet the application guidelines. Even I felt that there were some issues inherent in doing that, so I wasn't surprised when it was rejected. The world isn't that nice—that was one of the few useful teachings I had gotten during my life as a salaryman.

But occasionally, in the course of someone's life, some unexpectedly nice things will happen. After a normal greeting and a bit of small talk, someone from the Dengeki Bunko editing division who happened to see my work (it may not be necessary to hide their name, but following custom (?), I'll refer to them as M) asked me if I was Mr. XXXX who had written XXXX, and this deeply surprised me. The work I had submitted to the Dengeki Novel Award had the same settings as that one, but it leaned in a different direction as a sci-fi novel, and my pen name was an English name written in Japanese with phonetically similar kanji characters. M happened to have remembered my rejected work, so when they chanced across this work, which was on the Internet, their antennae perked up—hadn't they seen settings like this before? And that was apparently why he'd gotten in touch with me.

M seemed to have hesitations at making something that was free into something that was paid, and when I first met him, he was quite worried about what the Internet readers would think. I had thought about the same thing in the past, too. But the long economic recession and the downturn of companies resulted in limitations on overtime hours and an adverse wind blowing through the salaryman world. I felt that I'd need to find a side job if things kept on this way, or I'd have it tough. But if I did that, I wouldn't have any time to write novels. I can't say I *hadn't* been hoping to continue this work.

The world really isn't that easy, but occasionally something that is—a stroke of luck—is waiting for you. And of course, this luck is thanks to M, who got in touch with me to make this happen, as well as the admins of the "Let's Be a Novelist" website, who helped me in all sorts of ways even after it was decided—and above all, it's thanks to everyone who supported this work. I'd like to borrow this space to extend my deepest gratitude to you.

I'd also like to thank Mr. Kawahara, who gave more words of recommendation on my behalf than I deserved; Ms. Ishida, the illustrator, who gave this work much-needed added value; Mr. Stone, who did the mechanical designs; Ms. Suenaga, who did the color coordination; and all the staff who were involved with this book.

And above all, a deep, heartfelt thanks goes to the fortune that allowed me to deliver this book into your hands. I will work my hardest to ensure that this fortune doesn't end here, and that I can continue to deliver this work to you in future volumes.

Tsutomu Sato

THE LATECOMER FAVORITE

Reki Kawahara

W hen M, the editor in chief, started talking to me about writing a letter of recommendation for *that* *The Irregular at Magic High School*, I was overcome with excitement. "I'll write it! I'll write it. I'll write twenty thousand of them!" I answered immediately, though actually saying that to the editor may have been rather rude, or egotistical, or something... I'm not good enough to write recommendations or commentaries, so please enjoy reading something like a column instead.

Forgive me for prefacing this with a few personal matters, but my—Reki Kawahara's, that is—first book was published by Dengeki Bunko in February 2009. At the time, there were very few examples of novels released as amateur works on the web to be commercially released (at least, at the young-adult level), but in the past two years there has been an abundance of these "web-released" works that have been published by various companies, so I feel that the existence of online novels has been clearly acknowledged. And recently, the much-awaited publication from Dengeki Bunko is *The Irregular at Magic High School*, which I will refer to as *Magic High School* from now on.

All of you readers may already know, but *Magic High School* was serialized on the novel submission site "Let's Become an Author" starting in October 2008, and finished in March 2011—a very long work. It had sole occupation of the number one spot in the popularity rankings, and the page view counter showed an insane number exceeding 30,000,000 (!).

There aren't enough pages for me to even start detailing the appeal of *Magic High School*, which has garnered so much support. To try to sum it all up, I think this work beautifully and effectively employs a certain deviation that you can only expect from online novels.

Magic High School may have been written as a draft for a newcomer's prize application, but with its magical theory, constructed so finely it borders on tenacity, and its colorful cast of characters, who appear one after the other in the beginning, needing to cut it down to the required page count was probably inevitable. But in online novels, the only restriction is the author's limits. No matter how voluminous the settings may be, and no matter how many characters there may be, and no matter how deliberately and carefully the story develops, the writer can write to his or her heart's content.

Of course, this also deviates heavily from the theory in commercial business. Changing this deviation into appeal—and this is just my own opinion—relies entirely on the volume, or the amount of text in the work. Before I spoke of the author's limits, but the larger-scale a work becomes, the more difficult it is to continue it for very long. After all, the opinions of the readers are the only things giving the authors of online novels motivation (and in the beginning, you won't even have that...). A work will have shining charm precisely because the creator uses his or her passion toward the work as an energy source, and to take one step after another outside the realm of established theory.

Magic High School is one of those rare works that has flown high above those limits. The amount of text written by its author, Mr. Tsutomu Sato, exceeded the production pace of most occupational writers. For all of you who have been able to enter the *Magic High School* world via Dengeki Bunko, I very much hope you will continue to anticipate the infinitely expanding world beyond this book.

I've written a lot of formal sentences, but I'm pretty sure the best things about *Magic High School*'s deviating charm are the extreme love Miyuki has for her brother and Tatsuya's boundless invincibility!

I can't help but wait in anticipation for the continuation whenever I think of Ms. Kana Ishida's beautiful illustrations—whether she's making Tatsuya seem even more excellent and brilliant, or showing us ever more extreme behavior out of Miyuki.

The latecomer favorite from the world of online novels—that is *The Irregular at Magic High School.*

The Irregular at Magic High School

Tsutomu Sato
Illustration Kana Ishida

He is an irregular with an air of insight about him, and she is an honor student whose feelings for him go beyond the familial. From the moment the two pass through the gates of this elite school,

their peaceful garden of learning will be forever transformed.

Magic High's student council has recruited the brilliant younger daughter of the Shiba family, Miyuki, gifted with intelligence and beauty, to join their ranks. Meanwhile, despite his status as an untalented "Weed," her older brother Tatsuya catches the eye of the school disciplinary committee after he handily dispatches a problem. As both siblings rise to the upper echelons of the school's social scene, one thing is obvious: Their lives are about to get a lot more complicated.

VOLUME 2: ENROLLMENT ARC, PART II
ON SALE AUGUST 2016!

And check out the spin-off manga series, from Yen Press—*The Honor Student at Magic High School!*

Official Twitter!
(Japanese Only)

http://twitter.com/dengeki_mahouka

Frequently announcing new information and posting rough sketches!